MIDDLE SCHOOL
AND OTHER
DISASTERS

BIGGEST
SECRET
EVER!

BY WANDA COVEN

ILLUSTRATED BY ANNA ABRAMSKAYA

SIMON & SCHUSTER

First published in Great Britain in 2024 by Simon & Schuster UK Ltd

First published in the USA in 2024 by Simon Spotlight,
an imprint of Simon & Schuster Children's Publishing Division,
1230 Avenue of the Americas, New York, New York 10020

1 3 5 7 9 10 8 6 4 2

Simon & Schuster UK Ltd
1st Floor, 222 Gray's Inn Road
London WC1X 8HB

Simon & Schuster: celebrating 100 years of Publishing in 2024

www.simonandschuster.co.uk
www.simonandschuster.com.au
www.simonandschuster.co.in

Simon & Schuster Australia, Sydney
Simon & Schuster India, New Delhi

A CIP catalogue record for this book is available from the British Library.

PB ISBN 978-1-3985-2910-6
eBook ISBN 978-1-3985-2911-3
eAudio ISBN 978-1-3985-2915-1

Printed and Bound in the UK using 100% Renewable
Electricity at CPI Group (UK) Ltd

MIX
Paper | Supporting
responsible forestry
FSC
www.fsc.org   FSC® C171272

To my readers:
You are magical.
Love,

Wanda

CLEARING YOUR MIND IS EASY, RIGHT?

Today is my first advanced magic lesson with Mrs. Kettledrum!

Eeee!

I've been waiting for this day for what seems like *forever*, but truthfully, it's only been two absurdly long weeks.

The coolest part is that I am the **only one in my grade**—*so far*—who has *private* magic lessons.

One of my best friends, Sunny Akhtar, was a little bit jealous at first, but she and I had a heartfelt talk, and everything is good now.

Phew!

I totally understood how she felt. I know I would've been jealous if it had been the other way around.

These lessons are such a big step for me as a witch. All I've ever wanted is to be the best witch I can be, and now I'm on my way.

I'm positively buzzing with excitement as I walk across campus to Mrs. Kettledrum's classroom.

Is it possible that everyone and everything looks extra beautiful today? The sky looks bluer! And could it be that the birds are singing only to *me*? Everyone I pass either waves or says hi—even some of the upperclassmen.

I am radiating confidence and happiness!

When I open the door to the classroom, Momo, Mrs. Kettledrum's corgi, leaps off her puppy bed and jumps into my arms. She licks me all over, which is kind of *ew*, but mostly adorable.

Ever since I did an original spell that made Momo *talk*, she and I have had a special relationship.

Momo got to say all the things she'd always dreamed of saying.

Mrs. Kettledrum was super-impressed, and that's when she said I was ready for private magic lessons.

So here goes nothing!

"Are you ready, Heidi?" Mrs. Kettledrum asks. She winks because **she knows how excited I am.**

"I'm SO ready!"

Then I follow Mrs. Kettledrum into her office. Momo trots after us too.

"Have a seat, Heidi!" Mrs. Kettledrum says, and points to one of two cozy-looking chairs. I plop onto the middle of a blue plaid cushion.

"Are you comfortable?"

I bounce on the cushion. "Yup, totally comfy!"

Mrs. Kettledrum drags the other chair in front of me and sits down.

"Then let's begin. Lesson number one," she starts. "To strengthen your mind-reading gift, and to truly be a *great* witch, you must learn how to quiet and control your thoughts in any situation. Quick, successful magic can only be performed when your thoughts are calm and focused."

I nod vigorously, but I'm thinking, *Being calm and focused are not exactly my strong points.*

Mrs. Kettledrum rests her hands on her lap. She looks *very* calm and focused.

I'm pretty sure she never gets ruffled.

She adjusts her glasses. "The first thing I want you to do, Heidi, is to come up with a mantra to get your mind into a quiet, peaceful place."

I raise my hand. "What's a mantra?"

Mrs. Kettledrum shuts her eyes, like she's going into a trance or something, and then opens them again.

"A mantra is a word, phrase, or sound that calms the mind. My mantra is: *Peace and tranquility are mine.*

"It's *your* turn, Heidi. I want you to close your eyes and think of a mantra that will quiet *your* mind. Take as long as you need."

I close my eyes, but instead of getting quiet, my mind goes bananas.

Eek!

What should MY mantra be? I wonder.

What if I can't THINK of a mantra?

What if I think of one and it sounds STUPID?

What if I can't get this right?

In a matter of seconds I've gone from a confident, up-and-coming witch to a complete nervous wreck.

Chill out! I think.

Mrs. Kettledrum interrupts my topsy-turvy thoughts.

"Now, don't be surprised if your thoughts race around at first, Heidi. Simply take a deep breath. . . ."

Mrs. Kettledrum inhales slowly. "Think about something that will settle your mind. Your mantra should be a signal to yourself that it's time to be quiet. Simply let your mantra come to you. Don't be embarrassed or shy. There's no such thing as a *wrong* mantra. Just clear your brain of all distracting thoughts."

I shut my eyes again.

I'm glad Mrs. Kettledrum says that racing thoughts are normal. She also understands being totally embarrassed. That helps too. I feel a tiny bit less self-conscious.

Okay, what will my mantra be? Hmmm.

How about "Be quiet, Heidi!" No, too basic. What about "Turn off the noise, Heidi!" Or maybe I should be like a hypnotist, and my mantra could be "You're getting VE-E-ERY sleepy, Heidi!" No, I'm not trying to take a nap. How about, "Shut off your brain!"

Ugh, I'm so BAD at this.

"This is HARD," I declare, keeping my eyes shut because I don't want to look at Mrs. Kettledrum. **It'll just make me feel *more* embarrassed.**

Mrs. Kettledrum pats my knee with her hand.

"It *is* hard, Heidi, but **be patient with yourself.** It takes a lot of practice to get still and quiet. Let's try something else. Instead of starting with a mantra, I want you to **focus on your breathing.** Breath work is a handy tool to quiet yourself down.

"Please take a deep breath in through your nose, and slowly and gently breathe out through your mouth," she continues.

I take a humongous breath in through my nose, and slowly let it out.

"Not bad, Heidi. *Again.*"

I take in another dramatic breath and slowly let it out through my mouth.

I'm pretty sure I sound like an English bulldog snoring—or maybe I sound more like Darth Vader breathing.

And, instead of getting quiet, my mind wanders off in *another* direction.

This is no fun! I complain to myself.

I thought I was going to learn some REAL magic today, like making a mountain of candy appear out of nowhere, or whipping up a new wardrobe, or zapping a trampoline into existence. Or maybe magically getting a mini fridge for my room?

"*Concentrate*, Heidi," Mrs. Kettledrum reminds me.

I nod obediently and try to stop the rant in my head.

Focus, I tell myself. *You are a calm, no-nonsense witch. You can be 100 percent relaxed—even though you may not feel like it.*

You are as still as the water on a lake at dawn.

You are as calm as a golden sunset.

You are as weird as the biggest GOOFBALL ever. I open my eyes.

"I feel silly!"

Mrs. Kettledrum leans back in her chair.

Is she disappointed in me? I wonder.

Does she want to keep working with me?! She doesn't show any signs of being mad. . . .

Mrs. Kettledrum pulls off her glasses.

"What you're feeling is perfectly natural, Heidi. New ways of thinking can feel awkward at first. Believe it or not, one day you'll get to the place where every cell in your body is quiet. I didn't start out being calm in every new situation. It took years of experience and practice, but you have to start somewhere, and this is the start. Let's go back to thinking about a mantra."

I clasp my hands on top of my head. "What if I can't do it?!"

Mrs. Kettledrum smiles. "Of course you can, Heidi. Now close your eyes and try again. Trust whatever mantra comes to you—even if it sounds silly."

This time I don't let my mind spin like a Tilt-A-Whirl. And the next thing I know, something actually comes to me.

My eyes pop open.

"I've got it, Mrs. Kettledrum! My mantra is: *My peace is here and now.*"

Mrs. Kettledrum claps her hands.

"Well done, Heidi! That's a wonderful mantra! You've successfully taken the first step toward becoming a better mind reader.

"On to lesson number two: to do this step you'll need to turn your chair toward the window."

I stand up and spin my chair around. Mrs. Kettledrum shifts hers around too.

We sit down and gaze out the window. Students are walking toward the Barn for lunch. **My stomach growls.**

Glurrpity-gloop! Mrs. Kettledrum acts like she didn't hear it.

"Okay, Heidi, I want you to silently recite your mantra. Then focus on a student outside and ask yourself, 'What are they thinking?' After that, listen carefully for incoming thoughts. Ready?"

I sit back in my chair. Mrs. Kettledrum nods once. "Begin!"

My peace is here and now, I think calmly.

I have to pick a student and focus on what they're thinking.

Oh wow! There's Nick Lee! He's the guy who asked me to dance at the Halloween party! *He is SO cute!!!*

I watch Nick walk by. His thick, dark hair is swept back and reveals a slight widow's peak in the middle of his forehead.

One word: *adorable!*

Nick is a low-key crush right now. When I was crushing on Hunter McCann, I totally lost myself.

Luckily, or maybe unluckily, Nick isn't in the School of Magic. He's not in any of my other classes, either, so I hardly ever see him. This keeps me from crushing overboard. But I really want to hang out with him soon. I want to get to know him better.

Mrs. Kettledrum taps my leg.

"Heidi, put your eyeballs back into your head and stop thinking about boys! We all know what happens when you put crushes and magic together. Things can get very hairy! Clear your mind."

"I'm sorry, Mrs. Kettledrum! It's just that Nick is *sooo* cute! I won't let him distract me next time."

I jump back to attention.

Mrs. Kettledrum is such an amazing witch, she can see right behind the curtain of my mind.

When she says "things can get very hairy," she's totally referring to when I accidentally gave myself Rapunzel hair that would not stop growing, all to impress Hunter. It was a disaster of epic proportions.

Mrs. Kettledrum is right because I can't let a crush *crush* my dream of becoming the best witch in the world!

Mrs. Kettledrum looks at her notebook. She has no time for puppy love.

"Okay, Heidi, for homework I want you to practice quieting your mind. Really work on watching your thoughts so they don't wander." She hands me a sheet of paper with a bunch of helpful hints and goes over some of the details.

"Thanks, Mrs. Kettledrum. These reminders will be really helpful," I say when she is finished.

Mrs. Kettledrum rests her elbows on the arms of her chair. "Sometimes it also helps to imagine yourself in a calm place, like the beach, or any spot that makes you feel peaceful."

I light up. "I LOVE the beach! I never thought to go there in my mind!"

Mrs. Kettledrum looks at her notes again and flips the page. "There's one other thing I'd like to discuss with you, Heidi. I believe you're advanced enough to learn Emergency Spells."

I sit straight up because I want to learn *every* kind of spell.

"What exactly are Emergency Spells?"

Mrs. Kettledrum taps her notebook with her pen.

"They're spells for when something suddenly comes up or goes wrong—any kind of emergency that needs immediate attention. You won't always have access to your *Book of Spells*, so these are spells you can do on the fly. Here at Broomsfield Academy the staff of the School of Magic must come up with spells on demand all the time.

"So for our next lesson, I also want you to think of emergency situations where you might need to perform a spell on the spot."

I clasp my hands. "Well, that's an easy assignment! My life is a never-ending string of emergency situations!"

Mrs. Kettledrum laughs and shakes her head. Then she looks at her watch. "That's enough for today, Heidi. Remember to practice quieting your thoughts. You'll get better at it the more you practice. And I'll see you at the assembly tomorrow."

I hop up from my chair and move it back to where it belongs. Then I give Momo some kisses on the top of her head. She licks my cheek.

Slobberific!

"Thank you, Mrs. Kettledrum! I know I have a lot of work to do, but I feel like a better witch already."

Look out, world! Here I come!

TWO SCOOPS!

I trot down the path to the Barn. The Barn is where the student center and cafeteria are located—not to mention the bowling alley, the bookstore, the Secret Loft, and the Four Square courts out front.

One thing about becoming a next-level witch is, it makes you *really* hungry.

Hungry to learn more.

Hungry to get better.

And hungry for yummy food—that's because strengthening magic skills is a workout—a total mental workout, that is.

I need some brainpower!

I wonder if I'll see Nick at lunch today. I already know he's not at my table this week.

Merg.

And just my rotten luck, he *did* get assigned to Melanie's table. **Why does everything always go Melanie's way?** And lucky Annabelle is at Nick's table too.

Double MERG with a heaping side of MERG sauce!

Well, at least Sunny is at my table, along with Hunter and Isabelle.

Speaking of which, **those two are definitely a thing these days.** Everyone knows it.

And thankfully, I'm weirdly over it.
It's amazing how a new crush positively fizzles away an old one.

At the sandwich bar I order tuna salad on a soft roll, with cheesy cheddar chips, pickles, and carrot sticks on the side. Then I carry my tray to Table Five—my table of the week. Sunny slaps the empty seat beside her. **She always saves me a seat because she's a next-level friend.**

I set down my tray. Isabelle is on the other side of me, and **she's sitting next to Hunter, of course.** They giggle about something.

"What did I miss?" I ask as I sit down.

"Not much," Hunter says. "**But did you hear about the boy in my class who answered a pop quiz with a food order?**"

Confused, we all zoom in on Hunter as he launches into a story. This should be good.

"I'm not going to mention any names," Hunter begins. "But right now we're studying chemistry, and our teacher has been giving us pop quizzes once a week, and today was a pop quiz day. Anyway, our teacher starts spurting out questions and calling on random people, and he picks on this one kid in my class and asks him how the freezing point of water will change if salt is added to it."

"I know! It would decrease!" shouts another kid at our table.

"That's the right answer, but this kid wasn't expecting to be called on and yelled out, 'PEPPERONI PIZZA!' The entire class started laughing, even our teacher!"

Giggles circle around our table.

"Someone was thinking about what they wanted for lunch and not focusing on the lesson," Sunny says.

Hunter snorts. "Our teacher couldn't stop cackling, and he said he was going to have pizza for dinner tonight. It was pretty funny."

When we're all about done gathering ourselves together from our laughter, I think of another funny story.

"Hey, something similar happened to me this weekend!"

Now all eyes are on me.

Eek!

"Melanie and I were finishing up our homework when all of a sudden it was lunchtime, and she told me to take a break and come to the cafeteria with her. I saw her walk out the door, and I wanted to catch up to her. I grabbed my book bag and my library card, **and started walking out in my slippers!**"

"**Where did you think you were going, Heidi?**" Isabelle laughs.

"Melanie asked me the same thing, and guess what I said to her?"

The table collectively asks, "What?!"

"I said, 'Get your library card, Melanie, or they won't let you into the library!' I was so focused on my homework that I had no idea where I was going!"

Everyone giggles. It's normal to daydream for a few minutes, or get distracted and not concentrate on what you're doing. It happens to everyone.

"I guess the moral of both stories is: slow down and focus on what you're doing," Isabelle says as she wipes tears of laughter from the corners of her eyes.

"Wait. So what are we talking about? Pepperoni pizza?" I joke.

We all crack up again. These stories remind me of what I learned with Mrs. Kettledrum today. *Mindfulness is important in practicing magic, too*, I think. This also makes me recall the meditation techniques she gave me. I promised I'd share everything I learned in my advanced lessons with Sunny. I whip out my list and hold it in front of her.

"I had my first advanced magic lesson today, Sunny," I whisper, even though everybody at my table is in the School of Magic.

Sunny grabs the paper and studies it. "Seriously, Heidi? These are some of the easiest tips I've ever read. These tips are for *beginners*!"

This was *not* the reaction I was expecting.

I thought Sunny would be gushing with excitement, but instead she says my first assignment

is "for beginners," like there's
nothing advanced about it at all.
I try not to feel insulted. "Meditating is harder
than it sounds, Sunny," I tell her.

Sunny shrugs and hands the paper back to me.
"Okay, let's test it out soon."

I fold the paper and put it away. At the same time,
Isabelle gets up from the table. Before she leaves,
she taps me on one shoulder.

"Hey, Heidi, I really like your sweater."

I glance down at my dark purple cardigan. It's
nothing special, but Isabelle seems to think so.
She smiles at me with genuine kindness, like we're
really good friends. Usually we're just fringe
friends. We hang out, but mostly in groups.

But hey, I'll take the compliment.

"Thanks! I love anything purple," I say.

Isabelle is still beaming friendliness at me. Where
is all this sudden warmth coming from?
Does she want to get to know me
better or something?

"Plum is actually the hot color this season," Isabelle
goes on. "There's a whole article about it in *Fashion
Magic*, this trendy blog I follow. It has tons of
pictures. I can send you the link if you'd like?"

I pull back slightly, a little surprised.

But I'm not one to turn down compliments *or* friendly gestures—that's for sure! "Thanks, that sounds great, Isabelle!"

Isabelle looks pleased. "Good!" she declares. "Would you like to drop by my room after last period today? I have some purple headbands that would match your sweater perfectly. I'm happy to share one with you!"

I nod, because of course I'm not one to turn down **compliments** or **friendly gestures.**

Now I'm **really curious** as to why Isabelle is being so warm. She's always seemed pretty shy and distant. "That's really nice of you, Isabelle. I'd love to stop by later!"

Isabelle smiles. "Great! I'm in Dreamwood, Room 205. Meet me after seventh period."

I nod again, because why not? Though, I'm still wondering why Isabelle is being all buddy-buddy. Not that I don't like it. *I do!* It's fun to make new friends.

I watch Isabelle walk off with Hunter. Her dark curly ponytail swishes from side to side when she walks, just like Melanie's.

One word: *adorbs!*

As soon as they walk out the door, Sunny falls all over me. "What was THAT all about?"

I shrug like, *No big whoop.*

"Who knows?" I say. "Suddenly Isabelle is super-friendly."

Sunny sits back in her chair. "She was only super-friendly to *you*, Heidi. She's still shy and standoffish with me."

I nibble one of my chips. "She used to be that way with me, too, but maybe she's opening up. Maybe she feels more comfortable around me now. I do have that effect on people." I wink.

Sunny rolls her eyes and takes a bite of her grilled cheese. "Well, she's never been shy around Hunter—and now you. Promise you'll give Annabelle and me the scoop after you hang out with her later?"

I raise one eyebrow. "What exactly do you mean by 'the scoop'?"

Sunny shrugs. "You know—the lowdown. The dirt. The gossip. *HELLO?!*"

I frown.

Isabelle is barely a friend, and now I have to get some dirt on her? Sunny kicks my foot under the table.

"Come on, Heidi!" she pleads. "**There's a story here.** Think about it: Isabelle is pretty, smart, and athletic, *and* she snagged Hunter, who is one of the coolest kids in our class. **I, for one, would like to know more about this person!**"

I laugh. "Okay, okay, I'll see what I can do about getting a *scoop.*"

Then I pretend to be a news anchor with a special report. I talk into my fork, like it's a microphone.

"Wait! This JUST in! A shy, standoffish girl at Broomsfield Academy *liked* another girl's sweater today. The shy girl also invited the other girl to hang out after school. Everyone at Broomsfield is like, WHAT'S GOING ON? Does the shy girl have a hidden story? Tune in later for more juicy gossip . . . !"

Sunny cracks up. "Very funny, Heidi."

I laugh, and then I think, *I want a scoop too!*

"What's the scoop on Nick Lee? Do you know him at all?" I ask her.

Sunny raises an eyebrow.

"Why do you ask?" she says.

I roll my eyes like, *Just answer the question!*

Sunny smiles. "Okay, okay! All I know is that Nick is in my social studies class."

I clap my hands to show I'm all happy again. "Really?"

Sunny also rolls her eyes. "You'd better not have a crush on him, Heidi. . . ."

I hold my thumb and pointer finger about a half inch apart. "Just an itty-bitty crush. *I promise.*"

Sunny sighs and shakes her head. She still hasn't recovered from my last crush on Hunter. I totally get it. I went off the deep end, like, totally overboard.

Oh no! Here we go AGAIN! I hear Sunny think.

Sunny's thoughts are so loud that I can hear them without even trying—that's because we're such close friends. I tune in to her thinking.

I hope Heidi's crush isn't like her LAST one. She forgot all about me, and that really hurt my feelings. I hate it when she gets caught up in crushes. It makes me feel so left out! Heidi's one of my very best friends at Broomsfield. She's so awesome!

Aw, that is SO sweet! I think.

"I feel the exact same way about *you*, Sunny!" I tell her. "And don't worry, I won't get in over my head this time. I just want to get to know Nick a little better. It was fun hanging out with him at the Halloween dance. He seems really sweet."

Sunny pulls back and does a double take.

"Wait, did you just read my thoughts, Heidi?"

I nod because that's *exactly* what I did. "Yup!"

Sunny shuts her eyes. "Okay, what am I thinking NOW?" she asks.

I try to read Sunny's thoughts again, but this time I can't. "Sorry, Sunny, I can't do on-command performances. It's too much pressure!"

Sunny opens her eyes. "I was only thinking, 'Nick IS pretty sweet and cute!'"

I smile. "He is, isn't he?!"

We both laugh.

"Okay, here's the deal, Sunny," I tell her. "I'll give you the scoop on Isabelle if *you* give me the scoop on Nick."

Sunny hangs her arm across my shoulders. "Deal!"

Then Sunny points toward Melanie eating at the same table as Nick. "You could always get the scoop on Nick from your roommate!"

I roll my eyes once again, very dramatically. "I would *never* ask Melanie about Nick, or any other crush for that matter. She'd broadcast it *all over* school. I bet she'd hang a billboard with our faces on it. Or worse!

"She'd probably decide to have a crush on Nick too—just to spite me!"

Sunny shoves me playfully. "It's probably wise to not ask Melanie!"

I shove Sunny back. "Let's keep this whole crush thing quiet for now. I don't entirely trust Melanie yet. We get along way better than we used to, but our friendship is far from perfect."

Sunny puts her hand over her heart. "Promise."

Then Sunny gets up and slings her backpack over her shoulder. "I gotta run back to my room real quick. See you in class."

I grab my backpack too, and head to my class in the other direction.

As I walk along, I think about Nick and about how much I like all my friends at Broomsfield—and at home.

I feel very lucky to have so many friends. I'm also secretly excited about the possibility of having a *new* friend.

Will Isabelle become one of my besties?

Will she find her way into my inner circle?

Stay tuned!

THE FAIRY-
TALE DORM

Finally the school day is over!

I thought it would never end!

All I've been thinking about since lunch is hanging
out with Isabelle. Okay, I also spent *a little* time
wondering what Nick was doing.

Ack!

I have so much on my mind and so few
answers.

As I walk toward Isabelle's dorm, I'm excited, but
it also feels weirdly new, like I'm walking out of

my comfortable routine. I've never been inside Dreamwood, but I've heard it's a really cool dorm.

It's a sprawling Victorian house built in the 1800s. Everyone calls it **the *fairy-tale* dorm**—that's because it looks like an overgrown gingerbread house.

It has two supercool turrets with dorm rooms in them. There's also a wraparound porch where everyone hangs out on warm days.

The shingles look like rows and rows of white fish scales. The trim and accents look as though they've been piped on with a pastry bag, like swirly icing on a fancy cake.

This dorm is quirky, cool, and enchanting.

The wooden steps creak as I walk up onto the porch. Inside there are kids hanging out, reading, and watching TV. I head straight for the stairs that curve up to the second floor.

I have no idea where I'm going, but I figure the doors will have numbers.

I climb the grand stairs and walk down the hallway, which is lined with faded ornate rugs. Room 205 is at the end of the hall.

I take a deep breath and knock on the door. It swings open.

"Hey, Heidi! Come on in!" Isabelle says like she's truly happy to see me. "By the way, you can call me Izzy if you want. That's what all my friends from home call me."

"Okay, Izzy," I say as I start to walk into her room.

Then I gasp.

Isabelle lives in one of the towers, and the entire room is perfectly round—even the doors are curved!

I gape. I can't help it!

I have to take this all in.

Isabelle has a white iron canopy bed—
**something I've always dreamed of
having.** The iron bed frame is twisted with
scrolls and swirls at the head and foot of the bed.
Her bedding looks like a hand-embroidered doily,
and she has a bunch of white faux-fur pillows all
perfectly arranged.

One of her pillows is a fuzzy,
stuffed soccer ball.

Above the headboard is a **heart-shaped wreath woven with twinkly lights.** Underneath is a wooden sign that says **HAPPILY EVER AFTER.** All the windows have cream-colored velvet curtains.

Leaning against one wall is **a beaded silver mirror.** A cream-colored footstool sits by the window. From the middle of the ceiling **hangs a glistening white chandelier with dangling pink-and-clear dewdrop crystals.**

The light fixture looks like a candelabra, and the bulbs are shaped like little flames.

The other walls are covered with beautiful white-framed sketches and paintings. And if that isn't enough, Isabelle's room is a *single*.

She has this room all to herself!

One word: *astounding*.

"Your room is *unreal,* Izzy! How did you get a single in one of the towers?! It's like something out of a storybook. It's no wonder everyone calls this the fairy-tale dorm!"

Isabelle clasps her hands under her chin. She seems to appreciate my gushing, unbridled enthusiasm.

But maybe I should tone it down. I don't want to overwhelm a possible new friend.

Deep breath, Heidi. Have some self-control.

"Um, my family goes way back at Broomsfield," Isabelle explains. "In fact, this building was donated by one of my relatives, but that's not the real reason I got it. I actually requested a single long before school started. I had to write an essay about why I wanted a single too."

I wish I had thought to request a single! I think. But I'm not sure I could've written a convincing essay about why I had to have one. A single *sounds* great, but it might be lonely.

"So why did you want a single as a first-year student?" I ask.

Isabelle points to the walls behind me at the gallery of sketches, drawings, and paintings. "I like my own space to dream, draw, and paint. I'm kind of a private person."

I nod my head in wonder as I look at Isabelle's work. There are drawings of girls on the soccer team, and even a couple of sketches of Hunter that are a spot-on likeness of him. It looks like the work of a professional artist.

✦ 54 ✦

I cannot believe how talented Isabelle is. "Wow, you did *all* these?"

Isabelle curls a few strands of hair around her finger. "I did!"

I'm feeling a little starstruck and start gushing all over again.

"Izzy, you're such an accomplished artist—not to mention a super-great athlete—and your room looks like it was put together by a high-end designer.

"Are you, like, a goddess or something?"

We both burst out laughing. That last thing I said was a little over the top.

I'm such a doofus!

"I'm definitely *not* a goddess, but thanks, Heidi! And I'm glad you like my work—that means a lot."

Then Isabelle opens one of the drawers in her cute shabby-chic white dresser and pulls out a beautiful rainbow feather.

"This is the feather I chose at the Feather-Picking Ceremony. It represents beauty. The beauty of the world and all that makes life so wonderful—love and friendship—things like that. Mrs. Kettledrum told me that my power is to create beauty in the world. Watch this!"

I sit down on the edge of Isabelle's bed to watch. She walks over to a vase of daisies on her bedside table that are slightly wilted. Isabelle touches one of the flowers.

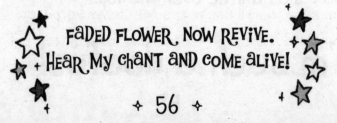

FADED FLOWER, NOW REVIVE. HEAR MY CHANT AND COME ALIVE!

Zing!

The daisy snaps back to life.

I clap. "Totally brilliant!"

Isabelle plops onto the edge of her bed. "Thanks! I'm not sure how I'll use my powers when I grow up, but I love sketching, painting, and fashion, so maybe one of those skills will help me decide."

"You could do anything. The world can always use more beauty and light!

"You could also be a pro soccer player! Don't forget that!"

Isabelle picks up her fuzzy soccer ball pillow and kicks it from her foot to her hands. "That *would* be pretty cool!"

Isabelle is amazing, I think. She's not shy at all. I am really looking forward to getting to know her better!

"So do you have brothers and sisters?" I ask.

Isabelle kicks the soccer pillow again and catches it. "I have two older brothers—*much older*. They graduated from Broomsfield a few years ago. They're the ones who got me into soccer."

She kicks the pillow ball to me, and I toss it back. "That's so fun! Does your family live far from school?"

Isabelle wraps her arms around the soccer ball pillow and hugs it close. "Well, we, *um*, they live very far away . . . ," she says a little reluctantly. "Luckily, I have an aunt who lives nearby, so I'll stay with her on school breaks."

Before I can ask another question, Isabelle looks at her watch and hops off her bed. "You know what, Heidi? I just remembered something. I have to finish this . . . *um* . . . really long assignment."

Then she quickly grabs something from her dresser. "Here's one of those purple headbands I was talking about." She holds a headband up to my sweater. "See? It matches perfectly, and like I said, plum is the hot color this season!"

She hands me the headband, which is really nice, **but I suddenly feel like a spell has been broken.** We were having such a nice conversation, and now **things seem different.**

"Izzy?" I ask. "Is something wrong? **Did I say something to upset you?"**

A worried look flits across Isabelle's face. It's only for a brief moment, **but I catch it.**

"No, Heidi, of course not! I'm . . . just thinking about my assignment, is all. Remember when we talked at lunch about getting distracted?"

Isabelle laughs a little, **but it seems forced.** "Ha-ha-ha, I guess that's happening to me now. Anyway, I hope you like the headband!"

I have a jumble of thoughts in my head, like laundry tossing around in a dryer.

Why does Isabelle suddenly want me to leave her room?

The assignment sounds like a convenient excuse.

Did I say something wrong? She mentioned she was a private person.

Hmmm, whatever it is, **she definitely doesn't want me here anymore.**

"Thanks so much, Izzy!" I say brightly, trying to quiet the questions swirling inside my brain.

Isabelle ushers me toward the door. I try to read her thoughts, **but I'm too weirded out to get a reading.**

Hopefully her change of behavior has nothing to do with me. **But it has to!**

Why else would she ask me to leave?

It was something I said, **but what?**

I go back over our conversation, but nothing I said was out of the ordinary. I just asked a bunch of normal get-to-know-you questions.

Or at least, I think I did.

I hope I didn't spoil my new friendship.

One word: *confusing!*

OM-BELIEVABLE!

Today we have an all-school assembly.

Magical students and non-magical students all in one place.

And I'm late.

I've been running late *all* day.

I was so late for lunch that my friends were already outside playing Four Square. That's when I decided to play Four Square **rather than eat.**

Nick was playing. How could I resist?

And Nick's really good at Four Square—just as good as Hunter and Isabelle.

After the game, I had to run all the way back to my dorm to get a jacket, and now I'm late for the assembly.

As I hurry down the sidewalk, I notice that nobody is around.

Everyone's already in the auditorium.

Eek!

What's this assembly about anyway? I wonder.

It includes upperclassmen, so it must be something BIG.

Maybe we're going to have a field day!

Or could it be another dance? That would be FUN!

I push on the door to the auditorium building. Sunny and Annabelle are waiting for me in the lobby.

I have such awesome friends!

"Hurry up, Heidi!" Sunny says. "It's about to begin!"

I pull off my jacket, because now I'm too hot. *Oh well.* "Do you know what the assembly is about?!"

Annabelle pulls off her backpack. "I heard it's a competition!"

My eyes grow wide. "Like a MAGICAL competition?"

Annabelle shakes her head. "I doubt it, since it's an all-school assembly."

Good point, I think as I follow my friends into the auditorium. We grab seats together and wonder about other possible school-wide competitions.

A poetry reading?

A doughnut-eating contest?

Campus cleanup day?

Throw a pie at a teacher contest?

Mrs. Kettledrum walks onto the stage, and Momo follows close behind. A hush falls over the auditorium when Mrs. Kettledrum stands at the podium.

That's when my stomach growls. It sounds like a motorcycle engine turning over. Everyone looks at me and laughs.

I'm mortified!

Sunny and Annabelle nudge me at the same time.

"Are you okay, Heidi?" Annabelle asks.

"Yeah!" I say, a little embarrassed. "I missed lunch!"

"Heidi, you shouldn't have skipped lunch! We'll grab some yummy snacks after the assembly!" Sunny says with a smile.

Did I already say I have *awesome* friends?!

Mrs. Kettledrum taps the microphone to see if it's on. The microphone squeaks. "*Gooooood* afternoon, Broomsfield students!"

"**Good afternoon!**" we echo back.

Mrs. Kettledrum goes over some routine announcements first.

She mentions the two soccer victories this week—both girls and boys.

Hunter and Isabelle must be SO psyched!

After the announcements Mrs. Kettledrum tells us the Broomsfield Academy Word of the Month, which is "loyalty."

She talks about what it means to be a good and loyal friend. "Loyalty is what makes friendships last a long time," Mrs. Kettledrum says.

Momo barks because she likes this idea. Everyone knows dogs are *always* loyal. They're humans' best friends!

Speaking of best friends, Lucy—my best, best friend forever and ever—is more loyal than anyone else in the world.

She will always be my best friend.

I hope I'm always a loyal friend to her, too.

I have missed her so much since moving away from Brewster and starting at Broomsfield Academy. We send each other letters every week and talk on the phone every weekend, but it's not the same. I can't wait to see her in person again soon.

Finally Mrs. Kettledrum puts her sheet of announcements to one side and takes off her reading glasses. "Now, I know you're all wondering why we called this special assembly today."

Whispers and murmurs echo throughout the auditorium. *YES! We ARE wondering,* I think. *And it feels like it's taking an eon to find out!*

"Well," Mrs. Kettledrum says, clapping her hands together, "I have *exciting* news!"

Sunny pinches my leg, and I pinch hers back.

"As you know, our school logo is over a hundred years old, and while we've loved it all these many years, it's begun to look a little tired and outdated. So the faculty has voted to create a *new* logo, and the entire student body is invited to participate in a school-wide logo competition!"

BROOMSFIELD ACADEMY

Everyone in the auditorium erupts into cheers and whistles. Sunny, Annabelle, and I look at one another and squeal.

Then Mrs. Kettledrum goes over the contest rules.

"These rules only apply to those of you who wish to participate in the competition. Please listen carefully. Come up with a simple, creative, and original logo to identify our school. Your design *must* include our iconic Broomsfield Academy symbols: a bear and a broom. Your design must also include the words 'Broomsfield Academy.' All design entries must be uploaded to our school logo contest page.

"The link is included on the handout you'll receive when you leave the auditorium. Each contestant is limited to *one* entry only. Judging will be based on originality, design quality, and visual impact.

"The winning design will become our new school logo! Good luck, everyone!"

We clap and cheer all over again, and everyone begins to talk at once as we get up to go. A logo contest is such a cool idea!

I'm sure fashion-mogul Melanie will enter. If anyone would want to leave a branding mark on this school, it's her!

I'll bet Isabelle will enter too. She loves fashion trends, and has the gift to make everything beautiful—which gives her an added edge.

Melanie or Isabelle could easily win this contest.

Annabelle taps me on the shoulder and snaps me out of my thoughts. "Isn't this logo contest amazing, Heidi? What an honor it would be to have your design become the new school logo! I'm definitely going to enter."

Sunny squishes in between Annabelle and me.

"This is a *once-in-a-school-lifetime* opportunity!" Sunny says,

handing us each a sheet of paper with the contest rules on it. "I'm totally entering too! Can you picture a sunrise in the background of my logo?!"

I laugh because that is *so* Sunny! She's not called Sunny for nothing!

"What about you, Heidi? Are you going to enter?" she asks.

I shake my head. Sunny and Annabelle each stick out their lower lip like, *Why would anyone pass up such an amazing opportunity?!* But honestly, I'm not into it. "I'm not much of an artist—so what's the point? Besides, I really want to concentrate on my advanced magic lessons. The homework is going to take a lot of my spare time."

Sunny's and Annabelle's faces light back up. I can tell they want to know more.

"I have a fun idea," Sunny says. "Let's go back to the dorms and talk about everything, including Heidi's new meditation techniques! Annabelle, is that okay with you if Heidi comes over to our room?"

"Of course," answers Annabelle. "Heidi is always welcome. She can move in if she likes!"

I'm happy my friends are so eager to learn more about what I'm doing in my advanced lessons.

It's perfect because I *have* to find time to practice so I can really perfect my mind reading.

"Sounds like fun," I say.

When we get to Sunny and Annabelle's room, I notice they've got some new stuff—three plush seats to be exact.

Actually, they're more like footstools, and they're shaped like mushrooms! They're short, super-fuzzy, and perfect to perch on.

One word: *supercute!*

The mushroom stools belong to Annabelle. She's been slowly decorating her side of the room, since she wasn't able to carry much over from England.

"I love, love, LOVE your mushroom stools, Annabelle!"
I tell her. "Where did you get them?"

Annabelle sits on a light gray mushroom. "Aren't they the cutest! I got them at Georgette's Folly, a super-funky boutique in Broomsfield Village."

"I *love* that store!" I tell her. "I may have to copy you! These mushrooms are not only cute, but they'd also be perfect for meditating on!"

Sunny bounces onto a cream-colored mushroom.
I hop onto the one that has a **red cap with
white spots and a white stem.**

It's squishy and *sooo* comfy.

"And you know what else?" Annabelle says. "**They
have secret storage spaces underneath
the mushroom caps!**"

I hop off my mushroom, pull off the cap, and find a
stash of snacks hidden inside my stool.

"Oh, YUM! Look at all these snacks!" My stomach growls again. My friends giggle.

"Heidi, I have some crackers and peanut butter or an apple, if you want that to hold you over for now?" Annabelle says.

I quickly pop the lid back on, beaming at Annabelle's offer. "Yes, some crackers and peanut butter, please!" I say.

After I eat my snack, Sunny gets down to business. "So, Heidi, tell us more about what you learned in your advanced magic lesson yesterday! Will you teach us something?"

I grab my backpack and pull out my meditation techniques. "Would you like to meditate together? Mrs. Kettledrum says meditation is the best foundational work for performing better and more *advanced* spells."

Sunny and Annabelle both nod eagerly.

"Okay, first we have to get into a comfortable position," I say as I pull my legs crisscrossed on top of my mushroom.

"Also, if you want, I read that you can hold your fingers in an *O* position, and then rest the backs of your hands on the sides of your knees." I show them how it's done.

Sunny and Annabelle follow my instructions.

"Wow, I kind of feel like I'm a yoga teacher," I say. "But maybe that's a bit of a *stretch*. Get it? *Yoga? Stretch?*"

My friends groan at my silly joke.

I look at my list to see what to do next. "Okay, now relax your shoulders and shut your eyes." My friends do exactly what I say.

I have such good students!

"Now breathe in through your nose slowly and then gently exhale through your mouth." We practice this together.

"You have to let your thoughts grow quiet," I continue. "It's not as easy as it sounds, so be patient with yourself. If your thoughts begin to wander, that's okay. Say hello to whatever song or words are in your head, and then silence it."

We practice breathing steadily with our eyes closed, except for me, because I have to peek at my paper again.

I skip the part about choosing a mantra for now. I take the more straightforward approach instead.

"Wow, this is hard, Heidi!" Sunny says. And I nod and look back at her like, *I know!*

"So Mrs. Kettledrum suggests chanting the word 'om' to help clear your mind. This chant is meant to help you feel more connected to the earth and the stillness of nature. **Repeat after me!** *Ommmm.*"

My friends mimic me.

"*Ommmm,*" Sunny chants.

"*Ommmm,*" says Annabelle.

"*Ommmm,*" Sunny repeats.

I jump in for a turn.

"*Ommmm . . .*"

"I don't think we are saying it right. **We sound like confused ghosts,**" Sunny says.

We all giggle.

"Ommmm," I repeat, trying to be a responsible instructor.

Sunny and Annabelle follow my lead for another round of *oms*.

"It sounds like we have bellyaches," Annabelle says.

More giggles.

"You see how easy it is to get distracted?" I say. "I told you, it's a lot harder to quiet your thoughts than you think. *Again*."

"*Ommmm . . .*"

"*Ommmm . . .*"

"*Ummmm,*" Sunny says.

I sigh. Why is Sunny switching it up?

"It's not 'um,' Sunny, it's 'om,'" I tell her. "Mrs. Kettledrum told me that this chant is very sacred, and that I should show it and meditation a lot of respect. So let's be serious! Keep your eyes shut, and everyone be silent for a moment."

My friends get quiet, and I'm just about to say *Begin again,* when my stomach growls *really* loudly this time. And it's way too funny.

We all fall off our mushrooms, laughing.

"I think I might need something more than just crackers with peanut butter!" I say, clutching my stomach.

Sunny hops back onto her mushroom and tries to get us going again.

"Yummmm . . . ," she chants.

Annabelle and I bust out laughing and roll around on the floor.

"Okay, forget it," I say. "I can't concentrate anymore because I'm starving. Anyone up for some real food?"

Sunny jumps up and grabs a package from her desk.

"I got a care package from my mom today!" She lifts a cookie tin from the box, pulls off the round top, and passes around the cookies. "Not exactly 'real food,' but these are her famous sugar cookies with rainbow sprinkles!"

I devour my cookie so fast, crumbs fly everywhere.

I brush the crumbs from my clothes.

Eek!

I make Cookie Monster look
well-mannered.

Then Annabelle passes around bottles of water, and
we catch up.

"So did you get the scoop on *Isabelle*
yesterday?" Sunny asks.

I squirm a little uncomfortably, but I also know that
Sunny and Annabelle want to get some info on the
so-called mysterious and standoffish Isabelle.

"Well," I say, wondering where to start, "she
lives in Dreamwood, **and she has one
of those tower rooms *all to
herself*!**"

"Ooooooh!" Sunny and Annabelle say at the
same time.

"Whoa, how did she get a room like *that* as a first-year student?!" Sunny asks.

I grab the sides of my mushroom cap and lean forward. "Well, she had to write a convincing essay about why she wanted a single. Plus, one of her ancestors, back in the 1800s, donated Dreamwood to the school."

Annabelle twists the cap on her water. "That's cool! So what else did you find out?"

I rock back and forth on my mushroom as I think about my visit with Isabelle.

"Well, I found out that not only is Isabelle a star soccer player, but she's also an amazing artist. She has an art gallery in her room! And all the sketches and paintings were done by *her*.

"She told me she picked a rainbow-colored feather at the Feather-Picking Ceremony. Her gift as a witch is making the world more beautiful, and if you saw her room, you'd see why that's her special gift."

Sunny and Annabelle stare at me like I'm a gossip machine. I can tell they want more—something *juicier*.

I decide to tell them about the strange part of my visit. "Isabelle and I were having a really great time. **She even told me to call her _Izzy_ because that's what her friends at home call her.** So if we're going to be friends, I thought I would ask her some basic get-to-know-you questions, like, where's she from? How many siblings does she have? That sort of thing.

"It went fine at first. She told me she had two older brothers who went to Broomsfield and that they were the ones who got her into soccer. But she didn't tell me where her family was from. She just said they lived far away.

"Then, _BOOM!_ All of a sudden she cut the conversation short and practically shoved me out the door. Isn't that weird? I can't figure out what I said to offend her. I've gone over and over it in my mind, but honestly, I can't think of anything. Do you think she may be hiding something?"

Annabelle leans over and grabs another cookie as she thinks about what I've said. **"Who knows?** Some people are just private about their families."

Sunny nods. "Annabelle's right. You never know what's going on in someone's home life. **Did you try to get a read on her thoughts?"**

I nod. "I tried, but I didn't get anything. **I think I was too flustered."** I shrug. "Oh well—so that's the scoop on Isabelle."

Then I look at Sunny with a wink. **"Did you get the scoop on Nick?"**

Sunny and Annabelle give each other another one of their looks. **Translation?** *Heidi and her ridiculous crushes!*

But Sunny keeps her end of the bargain. "Okay, my info on Nick is limited, **but I did find out that his favorite subject is** *history*."

I light up, because *hey, that's SOMETHING!*
"I love history too—well, at least I love the *history of magic*, but I can have an open mind to other types of history."

Annabelle flickers her eyes in that do-I-have-to-spell-it-out-for-you way. "Be realistic, Heidi! You're *a witch*! And you'll never be able to share that side of yourself with him, and that's a BIG part of who you are!"

"What are you saying, Annabelle?" I ask her. "That I should only make friends with witches and wizards? I can't have non-magical friends?"

Annabelle sighs. "I'm not saying that, Heidi. Not at all. But I *am* saying you're making things harder on yourself than necessary, like getting a crush on a non-magical boy. Which means you have to start out any relationship by keeping secrets from him."

I hang my head because I hate hearing this—even though Annabelle has a point. But being a witch has never gotten in the way of my non-magical friendships before, like with Lucy.

What I really should do is forget about boys altogether for now and keep focused on my goals as a witch. And that means learning how to control my thoughts and quiet my mind.

This restores my focus.

I clap my hands. "Okay, witches! Cookie break and gossip time are over! Ready to meditate some more?"

Sunny and Annabelle nod. We assume our meditation positions.

We relax—*sort of*—and shut our eyes.

"*Ommmm . . . ,*" I begin.

Annabelle giggles.

My eyes pop open.

"I'm sorry!" Annabelle says. "For some reason when I try to quiet my mind, all I can do is laugh!"

"Come on! This is SERIOUS! I want you both to think about nothing. I know that feels unnatural, but try. Now let's GO! *Ommmm . . .*"

This time Annabelle and Sunny *both* laugh.

"You know what? You two are *om*-believable!" I tell them.

Then we all burst out laughing.

Oh well, I think. Meditating with friends is fun, but it's totally useless. From now on I'll have to find time in my day to meditate all by myself.

I can do this! I can rise above all the noise in my head. I, Heidi Helena Heckelbeck, will leave a lasting magical mark on this world!

Of course, leaving a magical mark on the world is easier said than done. . . .

5

SURVEY SAYS!

After dinner I walk to the lake by myself to practice meditating. The sun has started to go down behind the hills, and the clouds are blush pink. I sit on a wooden bench overlooking the water.

Wow, it's so peaceful here—just what I need.

I pull my legs into the crisscross position and curl my fingers into *O*s and rest them on my knees. I close my eyes and slowly breathe in and out.

I repeat my mantra, *My peace is here and now. My peace is here and now.*

And for the first time, I actually feel peaceful.

Fish plip-plop in the water.

A crow caws above me.

I hear friends laugh and shout on the Four Square court, but nothing distracts me.

The quiet feels good.

Get used to this, Heidi. **This is the space where you can practice your best magic.**

Soon it gets dark and cool, so I make my way back to my dorm, Baileywick. The feeling of peace stays with me—that is, until I turn the knob and open my door. *Ka-blammo!* Melanie greets me with a rush of words.

"Hey, Heidi! I thought you'd *never* get here! I've been wanting to talk to you *all* day about the logo contest!"

And *ZAP!* Just like that my peace is gone.

"Are you entering the contest, Heidi?" Melanie asks.

I shake my head firmly.

"But why? It'll be SO fun!" she says.

I sit on the edge of my bed. "Melanie, you of all people at Broomsfield Academy know that art is not my best subject, and I have other stuff to focus on right now."

Melanie rearranges the perfume bottles on her dresser. "Well, I'm entering, and I plan to WIN! Did you know I already have my very own fashion logo for my clothing and perfume lines? Well, I do!

"And I got my inspiration from my mother's perfume bottles. They're always **so simple and classy.** She always says simplicity is better." Melanie shoves one of her perfume bottles in my face. "SEE?"

I take the bottle and look at it, because **do I have a choice?** *Not really.* And sure enough, Melanie has her own simple and classy logo—a cursive *M* on the label and a letter *M* gem hanging from the cap.

"It's really cool, Melanie." I hand the bottle back and sniff my hand. It smells like a flower garden in full bloom.

Melanie looks pleased with my approval. "It's fabulous, right? Don't you think I was born to create our new school logo?"

I nod because she wants me to agree.
"You definitely have a good shot at winning the
logo contest." And this is not phony baloney.
I actually believe Melanie could win,
but she'll have a lot of competition too.

Melanie jumps up and dances around the room.
"Just think! My design will live on at
Broomsfield FOREVER! Every time a student
buys a mug or a sweatshirt with the school logo
on it, it will be a tribute to *me*!"

Melanie is so over the top, I think.

"So do you have design ideas already?"
I ask her.

Melanie stops dancing. "No, not yet. But I will.
I'll start by studying the most iconic logos of all
time. There's such a rich history of logos!
I'm thinking of taking inspiration from my mother's
leather bags that she's had forever. She always
says her bags have survived the test of
time. And that is exactly what my
logo is going to do. They'll never
change it!

"That reminds me. Guess who's my study
partner in social studies? Nick Lee.
He's so supercute and nice."

I look Melanie straight in the eyes. "Melanie
Maplethorpe! Don't tell me you
have a crush on Nick Lee!"

Melanie shrinks back. "Whoa, calm down, Heidi! I just said he was *cute* and *nice*. I never said I had a crush on him!" Then her eyes narrow, like she's figured something out. "Wait a minute. I don't have a crush on Nick. But *you* do, don't you?"

Oh no! I've accidentally revealed my latest crush to *BIG MOUTH* Melanie Maplethorpe.

Aaack!

I try to keep my voice light and breezy. "No, not really. I mean, Nick is *okay*, but it's not like I'm *totally into him*. He's just a crush interest."

So BACK OFF! I add, inside my head, of course.

Melanie smirks, and I can just picture her filing my latest crush inside her gossipy brain under *Dirt on Heidi.*

"Well, don't worry, Heidi," she tells me. "I have zero time to crush this week between homework and creating a first-place school logo."

Our conversation is suddenly interrupted when somebody knocks on our door. We look at each other like, *Who could THAT be?*

Melanie is closer, so she opens the door. It's Jenna and another upperclassman. A girl I recognize from the School of Magic.

"Heyyyy, girls!" Jenna says in her ultra-cheery voice. Jenna is super-nice and the best RA ever. She and her friend walk into our room. "I want you to meet my best friend, Natalie Nguyen."

Natalie has black hair in a sideswept pixie cut, and her eyes are green.

She's really pretty.

What's interesting is that Jenna's NOT in the School of Magic, and yet Natalie and Jenna are best friends!

See? I think. *Magical and non-magical friendships—aka ALL relationships—can work.*

And that means Nick and I could totally be friends, *or even more!*

Three words: *Yes! Yes! YES!*

Melanie and I say hi to Natalie, who's holding a gold-plated pen and a notebook.

"Nat is going around asking questions to as many students as she can for her school logo entry. Since I'm an RA, I told her I'd help her survey some of the students on my floor," Jenna explains. "So what do you girls say? Do you want to help?"

Natalie and Jenna look at us hopefully. Interestingly, Natalie acts like she's never seen us  before. I'm sure this is because she doesn't want Jenna to become suspicious. Melanie and I play along. And when Jenna looks down the hallway for a second, Natalie throws us a wink.

Melanie and I look at each other. We are big fans of taking magazine quizzes, so this should be fun.

"Sure!" I say. Melanie agrees too.

Natalie's eyes sparkle. "Thank you! I'll just ask you both a couple of questions, and please answer as honestly as possible. Do you two mind if Jenna and I sit on your desk chairs?"

"Oh, of course!" Melanie says, jumping right into hostess mode. It's actually quite impressive. I roll my desk chair over to Natalie, and Melanie gives Jenna her desk chair. Then Melanie and I jump onto our own beds, happily waiting to be questioned.

"Let's start with you, Heidi." Natalie gets her pen and paper ready.

"What do you love *most* about Broomsfield Academy?"

"Um . . ." I think hard before answering, because my response would be, *The School of Magic. . . . DUH.*

But Jenna is here, so I speak in *code.* "Um . . . I really love all the extracurricular classes Broomsfield has to offer," I say as I return a wink to Natalie. She smiles and hides a laugh. She totally understood my code.

"What do you like best about our current logo?" she asks.

"I love the bear and broom, but it definitely looks outdated," I say.

Melanie nods ferociously in agreement.

"Okay." Natalie finishes writing her notes down before continuing her survey. "What do our school colors—yellow and blue—symbolize to you?"

"Hmm . . . yellow symbolizes sunshine, which shines happiness onto our school, and blue symbolizes peacefulness—bringing the students together in unity."

"Great answer, Heidi," Jenna says. She's always been so full of school spirit.

"Yeah, Heidi. These are great," adds Natalie. "Just one more, and then we'll go on to Melanie.

"What does the Broomsfield bear mascot mean to you? And what does the Broomsfield broom mean to you?"

"The bear is a symbol of strength and fearlessness. As for the broom, in the old days, Broomsfield farmers danced with brooms under a full moon to make their crops grow. Today the broom encourages the students to grow, blossom, and be fruitful too!"

As I keep answering Natalie's questions, I realize how much school spirit I have. I knew I loved Broomsfield Academy, but this is just making me love it to the power of infinity!

Concentrate, Heidi, you're almost done!

"Thank you so much, Heidi. Melanie, I'm going to ask you a set of different questions since I could see that you agreed with Heidi on a lot of her answers. Is that all right?" Natalie asks.

Melanie and I look at each other and giggle. It's weird how much Melanie and I have in common, and yet how much we *don't* have in common.

It can be baffling.

"Okay, Melanie, what should set our school logo apart from every other school?" Natalie begins.

"Uh . . . um." Melanie stammers a little bit, and I can see that she's having trouble finding a way to mention the School of Magic without actually mentioning the School of Magic.

"Well, um. Broomsfield Academy is unique because it's a regular academic school *and* a school that really focuses on teaching their students new abilities and helping them learn more about the abilities they already have.

"The bear and the broom symbolize all that, but without being so obvious and in your face. This sets us apart." Melanie smiles and nods. Proud of the code she created.

Natalie gets that same smirk on her face, but Jenna doesn't notice. Natalie continues, "What should our logo promise students who go here or who want to go here? And what feelings do you want the new logo to give you?"

"Our logo should tell our students that this is a happy and safe place to grow and become your best. And when I see our school logo, I want to feel proud, and I want it to make me say, 'I love my school! We're number one!'"

Melanie cheers and wiggles in her seat.

"Okay, last one. You have been so great! Both of you should feel free to chime in on this one." Natalie smiles at us gratefully. "If our school had a slogan, what would it be?"

Melanie and I look at one another, and suddenly I hear, *A magical future awaits you!*

For a second I think I just heard my own idea, but then I realize that I just heard Melanie's thoughts.

I give Melanie the floor. "Melanie, I don't have any slogan ideas. Do you?"

Melanie beams and pauses dramatically while we all wait for her answer.

"A magical future awaits you!" Melanie says.

"Good one, Melanie!" Jenna laughs.

"That was great, ladies. Thank you so much for your time. I'm going to try to talk to some other students before the end of the day. See you around!" Natalie and Jenna get up from the desk chairs and start walking out of our room.

"Thank you. That was really fun!" Melanie says as we wave goodbye, and she shuts our door.

"Wow, those were really great questions," I say. "Natalie sure is taking this logo contest seriously!"

Melanie frowns like I've just insulted her or something.

"Well, for your information, so am I! And I'm glad we answered those questions for her. Her survey gave me a lot of ideas."

Melanie shuffles through her desk for one of her notebooks and starts rapidly writing notes.

Who knows what she's writing, but at least she's starting to work on something.

I walk to our bathroom to get ready for bed, and when I walk back into the room, Melanie has on her pink-gray-and-white plaid pajamas and her pink fuzzy slippers. She sits propped up on her gazillion pillows, and the twinkly white lights above her headboard are on.

"I have officially set the mood to create my winning logo," she announces.

I grab my comforter to get under it. "You've got this, Melanie!"

I'm SO glad I'm not competing in this contest. What a relief! No extra pressure.

Our room is cozy and peaceful. Maybe I'm getting the hang of feeling calm.

Could this be a new me? Am I on the brink of becoming a better witch?

Survey says: *The future looks bright!*

A ROYAL FLUSH

Time for my second private lesson with Mrs. Kettledrum! We sit face-to-face on our comfy chairs in her office again.

"Today we will talk about Emergency Spells," Mrs. Kettledrum begins. "Heidi, have you given this any thought since our last lesson? Can you give me some examples of random emergencies, with the exception of injuries and illnesses?"

At this point in my magical career, I know that injuries and illnesses are in a different spell category altogether. Annabelle and Sunny are already pretty good at spells for healing. It is Annabelle's gift, after all.

And Sunny can harness the power of the sun to heal people. One time she healed me—in a matter of moments—of a sprained ankle.

Hmmm. I forgot to think of some random emergencies. Oops! I'll just have to come up with some right now.

Momo hops onto my lap and curls up.

As I pet Momo, the only random emergencies I can think of are things that have happened to *me*. But fortunately there are *a lot* of them.

"Breaking your mother's *favorite* vase," I start. Mrs. Kettledrum nods.

I continue. "Messing up a hair spell and having your hair grow without stopping. . . ."

She chuckles. "Great ones, Heidi!"

More emergencies bubble up in my head.

"Losing something, like the backpack charm I gave Hunter. Sucking up a cat toy in the vacuum cleaner. Or revealing a secret by accident. . . ."

Mrs. Kettledrum rests her hand on my shoulder to get me to stop. "Very good, Heidi! Those are all genuine emergencies—things that crop up more often than we care to admit."

I nod vigorously.

"So, now you'll begin to learn how to handle these little emergencies on the spot. Sometimes a witch just doesn't have time to sit down and pore over the pages of the *Book of Spells*. In that case, the witch will need a Make-It-Snappy spell!"

QUEEN of
Everyday
DISASTERS

Yes, this is exactly what I need! I think. *Because I'm the absolute queen of everyday disasters!*

Mrs. Kettledrum shifts her crossed legs.

"In *any* emergency, the first thing you should do is go over a quick mental checklist, like this:

"1. Stay calm. No matter how flustered or fearful you may feel, you must push these feelings aside. You can't do anything when you're freaking out.

"2. Ask yourself: 'What is the safest thing to do in this circumstance?' Also, if you need help, ask for it.

"3. Respond. Come up with an on-the-spot spell to meet the situation. Address every detail of the emergency in your spell. It's vital to be specific.

"Does this make sense, Heidi?"

I nod, understanding. "Yes, it makes perfect sense!"

"Good!" Mrs. Kettledrum says. "So, now we're going to create a mock emergency for you to handle.

"I want you to look into your backpack and find something—any object—and give it to me."

Momo hops down as I hoist my backpack onto my lap.

I fish around for something to give Mrs. Kettledrum. I pull out my favorite cherry lip balm and hand it over.

"Perfect!" she says.

Mrs. Kettledrum waves her hand over my lip balm, and it disappears.

Wow, someday I want to be able to do that! I think.

"Okay, now I want you to bring the lip balm back, Heidi," explains Mrs. Kettledrum. "What would do you do first?"

I press my finger on my chin.

"First, I'll go through my checklist," I say, and repeat the steps Mrs. Kettledrum just told me. "Once I've answered each question, I would come up with a spell on the spot."

Mrs. Kettledrum smiles approvingly. "Very good, Heidi! Now quiet your thoughts and come up with a specific spell that might bring your lip balm back."

I sit back in my chair and take a deep breath to quiet my thoughts. Then I close my eyes and think of an on-the-spot spell.

"Ready!" I say.

Mrs. Kettledrum nods. "Okay, now chant your spell out loud, Heidi."

I chant my spell.

LiP BaLM, LiP BaLM, hiDiNG FROM ME!
COME BaCK! COME BaCK!
ON THE COUNT OF THREE!
ONE! TWO! THREE!

I open my eyes and hold out my hands, expecting my lip balm to reappear.

But it doesn't. *Sigh.*

I look at Mrs. Kettledrum.

She raises one eyebrow.

"What do you think you did wrong, Heidi? What detail might be missing from your spell?"

I try to think of what might be missing from my spell. Did I miss an important detail?

"Oh, I know!" I shout.

Mrs. Kettledrum smiles when she sees I'm catching on. I sit back in my chair, shut my eyes, and chant my spell again.

CHERRY LIP BALM—HiDiNG FROM ME!
COME BACK! COME BACK!
YOU BELONG TO HEiDi!
ON THE COUNT OF THREE!
ONE! TWO! THREE!

Again, I hold out my hands.

SHA-ZING!

This time my lip balm reappears in my waiting hands.

Momo looks at me and barks her approval.

"That's right, Momo! I did it!"

I hold the lip balm so Momo can see it. "Wow! That was so cool!"

Mrs. Kettledrum gives me a high five. "And *that's* how it's done, Heidi.

"Always remember to include every important detail in your spell. It's the key to success. **Very good job!**"

I ruffle Momo's fur because **I can hardly contain my excitement.**

"Yip! Yap! Yip!" Momo cheers.

I love magic! I think. *I love this dog! I love my life!*

"Okay, you two," Mrs. Kettledrum says. "It's time for lunch. Let's meet again on Saturday afternoon at four o'clock."

"Okay!" I say, flattening Momo's ears back as I give her one last pat on the head before I go. Her brown eyes flash and her chubby body wiggle-waggles.

Momo is the world's cutest dog, and I'm so glad she lives here at Broomsfield Academy, so I can give her lots of pets.

"Bye!" I call as I head out the door.

Momo yaps.

"See you later, Heidi!" Mrs. Kettledrum calls.

I skip all the way to lunch, which may sound kind of corny, but I'm feeling it!

As I go, I wonder if Isabelle will be at lunch today. And more important, will she still want to be my friend after the other day? Or will she go back to being shy and standoffish? Maybe she's just one of those people who blows hot and cold, as my Aunt Trudy would say. *I hope not.*

I grab a hot turkey pita pocket at the sandwich station and a Granny Smith apple.

"Hi, Heidi!" Nick says cheerfully as I pass by his table. I say hi and smile, and Nick smiles back.

He just radiates niceness.

Did you ever look at someone and know in your gut that they are a nice person? **That's Nick!** You can tell by looking at him that he is genuinely sweet and sincere.

But he's sitting next to Melanie again today.

Merg!

Melanie waves at me, and it's like she's saying, *Look! I'm sitting with your crush!* I smile and nod to Melanie since I'm carrying a tray full of food. I also don't want to appear jealous.

As if!

When I get to my table, Sunny scoots over and makes room for me between her and Isabelle. Hunter is, as always, on the other side of Isabelle. He is completely smitten with her.

And great news! Isabelle is acting totally friendly and outgoing again.

"Hey, Heidi!" she practically sings. "So sorry to rush you out of my room the other day. I got really frantic about my homework all of a sudden."

I smile, because her words make me feel much better.

"No problem, Izzy! Homework makes us all a little frantic. So will you be participating in the logo contest? I can totally see you making amazing designs!"

Isabelle's face lights up. "YES! I've been working on ideas nonstop. It's so hard to commit to *one* design, but I'll get there."

Sunny jumps into the conversation. "I can't decide which direction to go in either!"

I decide to tell them about Natalie's survey.

"Last night an upperclassman came to our dorm and interviewed Melanie and me.

"She was going around surveying kids and asked all these great questions about how we see the school, how we want others to see it, and what would make the new logo stand out from the old one.

"The survey really makes you think about our logo's purpose."

Isabelle really loves the survey idea. "That is such a smart idea! And how cool that you got to talk to an upperclassman! Do you remember any of the questions that she asked? Maybe I'll even ask some people for feedback on my designs."

I polish my apple on my shirt. "For sure! I'll try to remember as much as I can and write them down for you."

Sunny taps my arm. "Would you share them with me, too?"

I chomp into my apple and nod. "Of course, Sunny!"

Isabelle taps my other arm.

Suddenly I feel like Miss Popularity!

I hope I can actually remember Natalie's questions and help my friends.

"Heidi, will you come to my room after classes so I can show you some of my logo ideas?" Isabelle asks. "I'd love to see what you think."

Sunny taps my foot under the table, and I can hear what she's thinking. *See, Heidi? Isabelle still wants you to be her friend. You should go!*

I tap Sunny's foot back, so she knows I read her thoughts.

"I'll be there! And I'll bring the list of questions," I say to Isabelle. I already know her designs are going to be amazing.

And it'll give me a chance to get to know her better, and maybe I'll learn why she *really* wanted me to leave her room the other day.

I don't want to be too nosy, but I still wonder what exactly happened. Maybe I will even be able to read her thoughts.

Later, after classes, I zip back to my dorm to sit and try to concentrate on the questions Natalie asked Melanie and me. I write down what I remember, and I write them down again on another piece of paper. I slip one of the copies under Sunny's door in her dorm on the way to Isabelle's. As I get closer to Dreamwood, I try to get into a peaceful, mind-reading zone. *You can do this!* I tell myself.

I hurry up the grand curving staircase and down the hall. The floorboards creak in front of Isabelle's door.

She must've heard them because her door flies open **before I even knock!** Isabelle greets me with a tub full of red licorice sticks. *YUM!*

"Want some?" she asks.

"Sure!" I say, reaching into the jar and pulling out a stick of licorice.

I bite into it, and my mouth is filled with that fabulous fake cherry taste that I love. "Thanks, Izzy! Red licorice and gummy bears are my absolute favorite candies!"

Isabelle bites into a piece of licorice too. "If I could only eat one food for the rest of my life, I'd choose red licorice!" she says. "Gummy bears would be a close second."

We laugh, and I forget all about trying to read Isabelle's thoughts.

Isabelle offers me a chair.

I grab **another piece of licorice** and sit down.

She plunks onto her footstool and picks up a pile of sketches. **"Ready to see one of my logo ideas?"**

I nod and blow into my licorice stick like it's a **straw.** Isabelle laughs as she hands me one of her drawings. Before I take a look, I give her Natalie's survey so she can read it later. Then I study the sketch, **and my eyes nearly pop right out of my face.**

"Heyyyy!" I cry. **"That's ME!"**

Isabelle's sketch shows me in a purple coat and matching hat. The hat has a logo on it—a bear, holding a broom, and sweeping.

Isabelle watches me as I look at her sketch. She is beaming with pride.

"So, what do you think?!" she asks.

I look up at Isabelle.

"I LOVE it! Is the logo one of your ideas for the contest?"

Isabelle nods proudly. "Yup! I'm going to draw more logos on things like pants, sweatshirts, and jackets, and get feedback from other friends too. The more feedback I can get, the better. Kind of like my *own* survey."

Isabelle grabs both of her knees with her hands. "You know what, Heidi? I think fashion may be my destiny. I love dreaming up outfits that will look great on people. It makes me so happy!"

She sighs dreamily.

"Now I just need to learn to sew! It's so tempting to use magic to whip up my fashion designs, but that would be kind of like cheating—you know?"

I laugh out loud, because I do know. It's the story of my life!

"I have the same problem, Izzy! I have to stop myself from using magic **at least three times a day,** and I fail frequently."

Little does Isabelle know, I planned to use my magical gift to read her mind today—a perfect example of using magic when I shouldn't, to get something I want.

I snap out of my thoughts when I notice Isabelle studying my face.

Oh my gosh! Why is she looking at me that way?

Can she read minds too?!

I look back at her suspiciously. But it turns out I'm totally wrong. Isabelle is just sizing me up for more fashion designs!

"You should wear more hats, Heidi!" she says, clapping her hands together. "And you're in luck because I just happen to have the *perfect* black hat for you."

I scrunch up my face, like *Hats? Really?* "I'm not much of a hat person, Izzy. I don't like the way they flatten my hair."

Isabelle waves me off. "Hats say a lot about a person. They say you're fashionable and cool, and they can also give you an air of mystery. And the best time to wear hats is when your hair might be a little flat already. You know, like on the day it needs washing."

I laugh. Hats on bad hair days *are* a good thing, but usually I just give myself a magical wash and blowout. Way easier than shampooing or jamming a hat onto my head.

But giving myself a cool, chic look— now that could be a different story.

Isabelle springs off the footstool. "Be right back! I have to go to the bathroom. But go into my closet. There's a box labeled 'hats' on the top shelf. You'll find a black hat in there. Feel free to try it on!"

Isabelle dashes into the bathroom—her very own private bathroom, of course!

But the biggest shocker is that she's letting me go into her closet *unattended*! It's like she just gave me permission to snoop! I race to the closet and swing open the doors.

I cover my mouth with my hand.

Isabelle's closet looks like it belongs to a movie star!

Or maybe a high-end fashion boutique.

How did she get a walk-in closet *at school*?

It's like a whole extra dorm room—*just for her stuff*—and Isabelle has *a lot* of stuff.

"Your closet is humongous!"
I call so Isabelle can hear me.

Isabelle laughs from behind the bathroom door. "These old buildings have lots of hidden perks!"

They sure do! I think as I study her closet.

All her clothes are hung perfectly by type: tops, bottoms, jackets, skirts, sweaters. . . . The clothes are also separated by color, forming a beautiful rainbow.

There are also backlit shelves lined with perfectly arranged shoes, soccer cleats, and really cool bags.

WHOA!

"Isabelle, your closet is *mind-blowing!*"

The toilet flushes. "Thanks!" she calls back. *What would she think if she saw the gowns?!*

I spy the box labeled HATS on the top shelf. "What did you say?"

Isabelle blows her nose. "I just said, 'Thanks!'"

And that's when I realize that I've just read Isabelle's mind!

I heard, *What would she think if she saw the gowns?!*

The water is running in the bathroom, so Isabelle must be washing her hands. I only have a few seconds to look for her gowns.

I push the clothes hangers this way and that, but I don't see any gowns.

Why does she have gowns, anyway? It's not like we have any red-carpet events at Broomsfield Academy.

The water in the bathroom just turned off.

Eek, I'm out of time!

I quickly reach for the hat box and pull it down.

Another big box comes flying down with it and tumbles onto the closet floor.

Oh no! I hope there's nothing breakable in there!

I hurry and place the box of hats on Isabelle's desk nearby. Then I lift up the lid on the box that just crashed to the floor to make sure everything's in one piece.

The inside of the box is lined in a beautiful cream velvet, just like Isabelle's curtains.

Set into the velvet is a sparkling tiara and scepter.

So cool! I think. *These must be left over from a play, or maybe even a Halloween costume.*

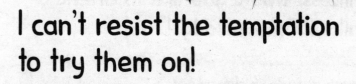

I can't resist the temptation to try them on!

I set the tiara on my head and grab the scepter. Then I jump out of the closet as Isabelle steps back into the room.

"Ta-da!" I shout, striking a pose in front of Isabelle. "I'm your friendly neighborhood princess! Would you like to attend a ball with me, milady?!"

I laugh at my own cleverness.

But for some reason, Isabelle is *not* laughing.

She buries her face in her hands.

Is she laughing really hard? I sometimes cover my face when I laugh.

Maybe she just thinks I'm *really* funny!

I turn and look at myself in the full-length mirror. "I've never seen such high-quality props, Isabelle! Where did you get them? Did you win them at a masquerade party or something?"

Isabelle uncovers her face. She stares at me sternly. Clearly she isn't getting into my princess gag.

"Heidi, please take those off!" she cries. "You're not supposed to touch them!"

I barely take in what she's saying because I'm too busy studying her magnificent scepter.

"Wow, this thing sure is *heavy*," I say, ignoring my friend's unhappy body language. "What's it made of anyway? It seems really old. It's beautiful."

And I just keep babbling on, while Isabelle stands there like a petrified statue.

"Hey, there's some writing on this thing!" I say.

I read the inscription to myself. *Presented to Her Royal Highness, Princess Isabelle.*

Wait, WHAT?

I look at Isabelle. All the color has drained from her face.

Then it dawns on me.

These are not *props*.

They're REAL.

Could this be why Isabelle didn't like me asking questions about her family?

And why she shoved me out the door the other day?

I think Isabelle may have a secret, and I'm pretty sure I know what it is. . . .

"Isabelle, are you a PRINCESS?"

MY LIPS ARE SEALED

Isabelle grabs my hands in hers. "Heidi, *PLEASE*," she begs. "You can't tell ANYBODY. Please, you have to PROMISE ME!"

My mind is a total mishmash of thoughts right now.

I'm reeling from the discovery that my new friend is a genuine, bona fide **princess**.

A royal A-lister!

I never dreamed I would have an actual princess for a friend.

I am equal parts **excited, starstruck,** and for the second time in an hour, **blown away.** At the same time, I need to support and comfort my friend, **who is completely freaking out right now.**

"I won't tell a soul, Izzy. I promise!"

Then I ask myself, Can I really *keep* this promise? A secret *this* big?

Eek!

And why would she want to keep such a cool thing a secret? I'm sure if everyone knew about this, Isabelle would become the most popular girl at school **overnight.**

"But I don't understand," I say to her honestly. "Being a princess is so special! **Why wouldn't you want anyone to know?"**

Isabelle's lower lip starts to tremble like she's about to cry. **She's in agony that I know her secret.** She flops onto her bed, flat on her back.

"I absolutely can't have *anyone* **find out about this, Heidi!"** She sits back up and begins to tell me about her royal heritage.

I listen with rapt attention, of course.

"Here's the story, Heidi. I come from an ancient royal, magical family, but we're no longer a ruling monarchy. The monarchy was done away with a long time ago because that kind of power wasn't needed in the magical community. Instead of the magical world being ruled by one royal family, the Council of Magic was formed.

"My family will always be lifelong members of the council because of our heritage, but now there are other voices besides just ours.

"So, truth be told, I'm a princess in *name* only. It's nothing but a formality nowadays—a nod to traditions of old. It's not like I'll rule anything in my lifetime—"

I butt in to try to help lighten Isabelle's mood. "But you *will* rule in the fashion industry one day!"

She laughs a little, and I hear some relief in her voice.

I decide to go on. "Honestly, Isabelle, **being a princess sounds so cool to me. It's hard to understand why you'd want to keep it a secret.**"

Isabelle lets her leg dangle over the side of the bed.

"I know it might be hard to understand, but think of your favorite person in the world, like, your very best friend. Now imagine if they only liked you because you're a *witch*?"

My best friend, Lucy Lancaster, has no idea I'm a witch. She truly likes me for *me*.

I know this because one afternoon Lucy actually knew I was a witch. She even had my powers for a few hours! But then due to a magical occurence called "The Forgetting," she didn't remember that this happened, and everything went back to normal. Thank goodness.

But I must admit it would be a total bummer if somebody liked me just because I'm a witch. How could I trust someone like that?

I give Isabelle a smile because I totally get what she's saying now.

"I guess it would stink if somebody only liked you because you're a princess. . . ."

Isabelle grabs her soccer pillow and hugs it close. "Exactly! And the whole reason I chose to come to Broomsfield Academy without a title is so I could be a *normal* magical student.

"Trust me. If everyone knew I came from a royal family of witches and wizards, they'd want to know me for all the wrong reasons. They'd probably want special favors, too, like trying on my tiaras or wielding my scepter."

We both giggle. I take off the tiara.

"Well, I've heard that fame can do weird things to people," I admit. "You'd probably never know who you could trust.

"I always imagined that being royalty like a princess would make your life easier. I guess I never thought it could make your life so much more difficult!"

Isabelle sighs. "Yup."

"Does the school know about your background?" I ask.

Isabelle nods. "Oh yeah. The administrators know everything about my family history, but they also respect my wish to keep my background quiet."

I'm still bubbling over with questions. "Does Hunter know?"

Isabelle's eyes grow wide again.

"No way, Heidi!

"I don't want any of the students at Broomsfield Academy to know, especially Hunter. I want him to like me for *me*—not just because I'm a princess. If Hunter found out, that would be the worst!"

I carefully lay the tiara and scepter back in the velvet-lined case. "Well, if I were a princess, I'd have a really hard time keeping it a secret.

"I'd want *everyone* to know. I'd probably blab it all over the place."

Isabelle shakes her head firmly. "Believe me, Heidi, *you wouldn't.* So please will you *promise, promise, PROMISE* to keep my secret?!"

I cross my heart. "Don't worry, Isabelle. My lips are sealed, and I *promise, promise, PROMISE,* your secret is safe with me."

Isabelle flops back onto her bed in relief.

"Thanks, Heidi. You have no idea how much that means to me."

Then Isabelle bounces back up and makes a dash for her box on the desk—the box I was supposed to get—and rummages through it. She pulls out a black fedora.

"Voila!" she cries. "*This* is the hat I was talking about." She hands it to me.

I pop it onto my head, and it fits perfectly.

I walk over to her mirror and look at the hat from all sides. It certainly makes me look cool and mysterious.

Isabelle claps her hands. "I knew it would look amazing on you! It's so striking with your red hair too! You must keep it!"

I tip the hat to one side. "Are you sure?"

Isabelle nods enthusiastically. "*Absolutely!*

"I never wear it, **and it looks way better on you than it does on me.**"

Isabelle grabs her soccer cleats. "Hey, I have to head to practice now." She looks at me. "**And, Heidi, thank you again for keeping my secret. You are a good friend.**"

I grab my stuff, and we walk out together.

I still can't believe Isabelle is a princess.

The only downside is, **now** I have to keep this humongous secret.

Help!

Sunny wanted the scoop on Isabelle, and wow, what a scoop this would be!

I promised Isabelle I would keep her secret, but this is too much of a secret for one girl to handle!

I'm positively bursting! What am I going to do now?

Two words: *I'm doomed.*

8

STICKY FINGERS!

Carrying around top secret information is a lot harder than it sounds.

You'd think it would be easy for me, since I've kept the secret of my being a witch from so many people over the years.

But this is different.

My family knows I'm a witch, so I can talk to them about it. NO ONE knows this secret, and I want to tell someone so badly!

I imagine opening a window, leaning out of it, and screaming at the top of my lungs, *ISABELLE SUMMER IS A PRINCESS!!!*

It's like a nagging, persistent itch that screams, *Scratch me!* Or in my case, *Spill it!*

But I know that nothing good would come of telling Isabelle's secret.

Ugh!

I'm not programmed to carry this kind of information! I wish I had never accidentally knocked over that box with Isabelle's tiara and scepter.

I feel like a ticking time bomb that may go off at any moment.

I have to be strong!

As I walk across campus, I spy Jenna's best friend, Natalie, sitting on the steps of her dorm. Maybe I should go say hi. It might help get my mind off this burdensome secret.

"Hey, Natalie!"

Natalie looks up from a stack of papers she's reading—probably all her notes from her surveys. "Hey, Heidi, what's up?"

I sit down beside her. "Not much. Have the surveys been helpful?"

Natalie nods. "So helpful. The answers have given me a clear idea of what students think about Broomsfield Academy. Now I can design a logo that really sums up the spirit of our school. Thanks again for taking the time to answer my questions."

I smile. "Anytime, Natalie!" Then I tell her I shared the survey idea with Isabelle and how it inspired her to get feedback for her own logo designs.

"That's great, Heidi! I'm glad you shared my idea with another magical student," she says. "And hey, I owe you and your roommate, Melanie, one for acting like you didn't know me when Jenna brought me to your room the other night. Jenna doesn't know I'm a witch. **That's top secret info!**" She pretends to zip her lips with her fingers.

I laugh, and it occurs to me that **witches have to keep *a lot* of secrets** about their **magical abilities.** And now I have Isabelle's big secret weighing on me.

"How long have you and Jenna been friends?" I ask.

Natalie shoves her notes into her backpack. "Since elementary school, and I've kept my secret from her all this time."

Wow. I've known Lucy since elementary school too! "My best friend from elementary school isn't a witch either, and I've had to keep the same secret. Sometimes it's hard. How have *you* done it all these years?"

Natalie shrugs. "I've kept my secret from Jenna for so long that it's pretty easy now, but some secrets are easier to keep than others. It takes a lot of discipline to keep a secret. Luckily, the School of Magic teaches us how to fix things when we slip up. You'll see!"

Natalie stands up to go, so I do the same. "Tell your friend good luck in the logo competition!" she says.

I walk down the steps. "I will! Good luck to you too, Natalie. And thanks for chatting!"

She waves as she walks away.

Sigh.

Now I'm alone again with this whopping secret.

Natalie wasn't kidding when she said some secrets are easier to keep than others.

Hmmm, I wonder if I can erase Isabelle's secret from my memory with magic.

Nah, too risky! What if I accidentally erase *other* information in my brain at the same time? Besides I *WANT* to know this secret.

What I *don't* want is to spill the beans.

Then it hits me: *Why don't I call Lucy?!*

I can tell Lucy my secret because she doesn't know Isabelle! That would take such a load off my mind.

There is, however, one teensy-weensy problem. It's Thursday, and we don't get our phones back for the weekend until Friday after classes.

MERG!!!

There's absolutely no way I can wait that long!

I *have* to get this off my mind right now!

Maybe I can just tell Mrs. Kettledrum I have to make an emergency call to my mom. Mrs. Kettledrum will understand.

Okay, that settles it. I'll go ask her right now!

I pick up my pace, and then I break into a run all the way to Mrs. Kettledrum's apartment, which thankfully is in my dorm.

I knock on the door and wait.

No answer.

I knock again.

Nothing.

One more knock.

Ugh! She's not home!

Then I get another idea. Maybe I can sneak into Mrs. Kettledrum's apartment and *borrow* my phone for a few minutes.

This might be better than my first idea! Then I wouldn't have to make up a reason why I need to use my phone.

I try the doorknob. It's locked.

Maybe you should try an Emergency Spell? I suggest to myself. *This is, after all, an emergency!*

I bite my thumbnail for a second as I think this through.

Don't worry, Heidi! No one will ever know!

Besides, it's not like you're breaking and entering— you're just practicing your homework!

And just like that, I convince myself to fall for my own harebrained idea.

I check the hallway both ways. No one is around, and there's not so much as a footstep anywhere to be heard. I make up a spell on the spot.

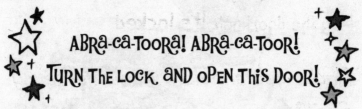

ABRa-ca-TooRa! ABRa-ca-TooR!
TuRN THe Lock, aND oPeN THis DooR!

CLICK!

The door swings open!

Well, THAT was easy!

But there's no time to admire my dazzling on-the-spot spell. I must find the basket that holds all the cellphones. I scan the room like some frantic thief.

Ah, there it is! I think, spying the basket on top of a bookshelf.

I reach for the basket and pull it down. This reminds me of raiding the cookie jar when you're not supposed to, **but you do anyway.**

I dig through the phones.

Where are you? Where are you?

Oh, *THERE YOU ARE!*

It's a good thing I put a gummy
bear sticker on the back of my
phone or it would've taken
a lot longer to find it.

I clutch my phone and dash out the
apartment door, shutting it behind me. My heart
knocks against my ribs as I think
about my next move.

*Where can I talk privately without
getting caught?* I wonder.

Melanie might be in our room, so that's out.

The Secret Loft in the Barn is too far
away.

Then I spy a closet down the hall.

Perfect.

I race to the closet, sneak inside, and flick on the light.

It's small, but it'll do! I flip over an empty cleaning bucket, sit down, and dial Lucy's number.

I shake one hand back and forth as I wait for Lucy to answer. Her phone keeps ringing and ringing until her message comes on. *Oh, Lucy! Why aren't you there? Don't you know I NEED you right now?* I tap end.

Suddenly I become very aware that I'm sitting inside a broom closet with an off-limits— somewhat stolen—phone and a headful of angst.

What is WRONG with me?!

Woop! Woop! Woop!

I fly off the bucket when my phone suddenly rings.

Woop! Woop! Woop!

I have the red-alert ringtone for Lucy. **And right now it sounds more like a siren.** I answer.

Eek, I hope nobody heard!

"Heidi? Did you just call?" Lucy asks.

I grip my phone. **"I DID!"** I say as quietly as possible. **"I *had* to talk to you!"**

I maneuver myself back onto the bucket.

"Is everything okay, Heidi?" Lucy asks. "Are you all right? How'd you get your phone on a weekday?"

I cup the speaker with my hand to muffle my voice. "Everything's okay, except for one major thing," I tell her.

"What?" Lucy says with concern in her voice.

I have to quickly relieve Lucy's fear. It's not like I'm injured or anything. "My new friend Isabelle told me this ginormous secret today, and I don't think I can keep it to myself.

"Oh, LuLu! It's *such* a juicy secret! All I want to do is dish about it. Can I tell you, since you don't even know her?"

Lucy's quiet on the other end.

Why doesn't she *say* something?!

"But, Heidi, what if I *do* meet Isabelle someday?" she asks. "Then what am I supposed to do?"

I hadn't thought of that, but the chances of Lucy and Isabelle meeting are pretty slim, unless Lucy decides to go to Broomsfield Academy, which isn't totally out of the question. "Well, if I can't tell *you*, then who *can* I tell? *Please, Lucy!* I need to get this secret out of my system!"

Lucy sighs loudly. "Trust me, Heidi. If you tell me her secret, you're going to regret it. The basic rule of friendship is never to betray a friend's trust. What if I did something like this to *you*?"

Ouch! I would hate it if Lucy ratted me out on something personal.

Now I officially feel rotten on two counts.

I feel guilty about keeping my witch identity from Lucy in the first place. And I feel guilty for wanting to tell Isabelle's secret.

But Isabelle's secret is different from mine. Witches and wizards can't reveal their true identities for so many reasons, the biggest one being that for millennia they have worked in secret without the rest of the world knowing that they really exist.

Isabelle's secret, on the other hand, is a noble secret—no pun intended—as well as a personal secret to protect herself.

I understand this, but I still don't know how I'm going to keep it.

"Heidi, are you still there?" Lucy says.

Oops! I got lost in my thoughts.

"Sorry, Lucy! I'm here! Are you sure I can't tell you my secret so I can stop obsessing?"

Lucy sighs. "I'm sure, Heidi. Just be disciplined. The urge to spill will die down in a few days."

I'm about to say something else when I hear footsteps in the hall. "Someone is coming, Lucy! Gotta go! Miss you lots!" I hang up and jam the phone into my pocket.

The footsteps stop in front of the closet door.

I freeze like an opossum playing dead.

I'm so scared, I can't breathe.

Uh-oh!

The doorknob is turning! My cover is about to be blown! I squeeze my eyes shut.

"Heidi, what are you *doing* in here?"

I open my eyes. It's Jenna.

"Uh, n-nothing much," I stammer. "I just needed a quiet place to practice my meditating."

Jenna rolls her eyes. "Come on, Heidi. I heard you talking to someone."

My eyes shift to the left.

Do I look guilty or what?

"Um, I was just chanting my mantra. That's all!"

Jenna jerks her thumb back toward the hallway. "Get going," she says like she doesn't totally believe me. "Or you'll be late for dinner."

I hop up off the bucket, turn off the light, and *skedaddle*—as my dad would say when he wants me to move it.

I'm pretty sure Jenna thinks I'm up to something. I'm probably the only student she's ever found sitting in a broom closet talking to herself.

But what she doesn't know is that I'm dealing with a real-life emergency, and sometimes that involves doing things that are out of the ordinary.

And now I'm stuck with my phone, which feels more like a hot potato.

I take it out of my pocket, turn it off, and hide it in my backpack. **There's no way I'm going to return it to Mrs. Kettledrum's basket now.** I can't take any more angst today. Hopefully Mrs. Kettledrum won't notice that my phone is missing.

On the way to dinner, I think more about what Lucy said. **I need to exercise discipline.**

Since when did Lucy get so much more mature than me? I sigh.

She was always more mature than me. **Most people are!**

Ugh, why is discipline so HARD?

And why does this topic keep cropping up?!

It seems like discipline is the answer to everything.

I have to exercise discipline in my meditation practice.

I have to be disciplined so I don't overuse magic.

And now I have to rely on discipline to keep a humongous secret.

One word: *BLAH!*

Discipline is *not* fun.

It feels more like a form of punishment. But somehow I know deep down that discipline is the key to success.

Without it I'll never become the best witch, or a trusted friend, or even a good student.

Still, the urge to blab about Isabelle's secret is *SO* intense.

Will I make it to tomorrow morning without spilling the beans? And then the day after that? And the day after that?

Yes! I think.

You can do this, Heidi. . . .

Well, at least I hope I can!

LOOSE LiPS

So far I've kept my lips sealed through an **entire**
night *and* a whole school day. And I'm happy to
say, Isabelle's secret is still safe.

I deserve a medal!

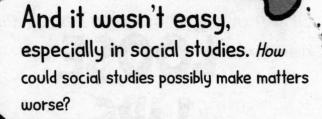

And it wasn't easy, especially in social studies. *How could social studies possibly make matters worse?*

Because today we started a unit on England, **and talked about the British royal family!**

Seriously!

Of ALL the subjects, why royalty? Why today?

On the bright side, this subject has helped me in a weird way too.

It's allowed me to talk about royalty in a roundabout manner, and *this* has let a little air out of my balloon of a secret, if you know what I mean.

At lunch we gabbed all about Queen Elizabeth. Who knew she owned more than thirty corgis in her lifetime?!

She also visited more than a hundred countries and made over twenty-one thousand appearances during her seventy-year reign. I mean, *wow*!

I was also a little surprised when Isabelle bravely jumped into the conversation.

It was kind of weird, too.

She gave a mini sermon—most likely directed at me—about Queen Elizabeth's best qualities: steadfastness, loyalty, devotion, respect, and discipline.

These, of course, are my *worst* qualities.

It really felt like Isabelle was listing them for my benefit only, like these are the qualities I'd better have to keep her secret—or else!

And that word. "Discipline." It popped up AGAIN.

I feel like I need to tell the universe that I've got this.

I know I *have* to keep my mouth shut.

And that's not all.

Our social studies assignment for the weekend
is to write an essay about what it would
be like to be a prince or a princess for
a day.

I'm not even kidding. This
is our real honest-to-goodness
assignment.

Sigh.

If I were a princess, I would **definitely**
want a fairy godmother. And if I *did* have
a fairy godmother, she would say, *Heidi, it's
Friday night! You can forget all
your troubles!*

And POOF! It actually *is* Friday night, and
that means movie night in Mrs. Kettledrum's
apartment! *Yippee!*

Melanie and I throw on our favorite pajamas and bathrobes. I remember that Mrs. Kettledrum said she'd return all our phones at movie night. I shove my phone into my bathrobe pocket so I can hopefully sneak it back.

Shhh.

Whisp! Whisp! Whisp! Our slippers scuff the floors as Melanie and I race down the hallway.

We want to get there early so we can get the best seats.

"Hello, girls!" Mrs. Kettledrum sings. And since we are early, she asks us to help her make popcorn.

Melanie places pillows on the sofa to save the best seats in the house for us. Then she runs into the kitchen to join Mrs. Kettledrum, and I casually lag behind them.

As soon as Melanie and Mrs. Kettledrum have their backs toward me, I run across the room and toss my phone back into the cell phone basket.

Whew! I did it!

Then I zoom into the kitchen. My heart is thwacking against my ribs again.

"Heidi, why is your face so red?" Melanie asks as she puts a bag of popcorn into the microwave. "Do you feel okay?"

I put my hands on my cheeks. They're definitely warm, but I'm not about to admit that it's because I'm a low-key criminal. "Oh, it's just from running down the hall. No biggie!"

Melanie shrugs.

Mrs. Kettledrum hands me a plate of chocolate chunk cookies. One of her eyebrows is raised. Does that mean she somehow knows I took—I mean, borrowed— my phone?

I turn on my heel and hightail it back into the living room. I place the cookie plate on the coffee table and plunk onto the couch.

I need a moment to recover from Mrs. Kettledrum's suspicious look and from returning my borrowed phone.

Ugh, am I a bad person? I ask myself.

Not REALLY.

I mean, sometimes I might do something I'm not supposed to. Possibly too often.

Actually, only when I'm in a jam. But I'm often in a jam.

Soon other kids begin to show up and grab seats as I ponder my dilemma. Melanie flumps onto the couch beside me. She hands me a bowl of popcorn and rests her own on her lap.

"So what's the movie tonight?" Melanie asks. Mrs. Kettledrum always keeps the movie a secret until showtime.

Mrs. Kettledrum stands in front of the screen and clasps her hands together. "Well, gang! I'm happy to announce that tonight's movie *is The Princess Diaries*!"

Everybody claps and cheers—everyone, that is, except *me*.

Of *all* the movies, why did she have to pick *THIS* one!

Is she seriously KIDDING ME RIGHT NOW?!

A princess movie when I have a full-blown princess secret?

And on top of an assignment on royalty?

Why does this keep happening?

How can I watch a movie about the *one* thing I can't get off my mind?

I want to scream all the way down the hall to my room. But instead I sit frozen in angst on the couch.

Nobody around me has any idea my thoughts are totally out of control right now.

I look around the room. Everyone else looks so happy and carefree, with not a single worry in the world!

But not me. I'm being held captive by a secret!

And did I mention that having a secret this big is weirdly lonely?

It's like being on a deserted island
with no one to talk to.

Help!

S.O.S., I think as I pop a piece of popcorn
into my mouth.

The popcorn goes down my throat the wrong way, of course, and makes me cough and sputter. Melanie hands me a water bottle. I take a sip. My eyes are watering. Now my face is probably as red as my hair.

Calm down, Heidi. Just calm down! I say, trying to soothe myself.

The movie selection is an odd coincidence. Just enjoy it for what it is.

Okay, okay!

So that's what I do. And even though I've seen *The Princess Diaries* before, this time I see the movie through Isabelle's eyes.

When the main character, Mia, finds out she's a princess, her life dramatically changes overnight. The popular kids suddenly take notice of her, and they all want to be her best friend.

Even the most popular guy in school breaks up with his girlfriend so he can go out with Princess Mia.

But Mia doesn't get swept up in the attention. She stays true to herself, just like Isabelle.

More and more I begin to see why Isabelle doesn't want people to know her secret. I mean, look what it's done to *me*?!

After the movie Mrs. Kettledrum hands each girl her cell phone as we leave. Melanie and I head back to our room, and guess what we talk about? Royalty stuff, of course.

"So how do you like our social studies assignment?" Melanie asks.

I shrug. "It's okay, I guess."

"Are you kidding?" Melanie says dramatically. "This is the best assignment we've *ever* had! I've always dreamed about being a princess! If I got to be a princess for a day, I would have a perfect wardrobe, perfect hair, perfect accessories, and TONS of sparkly diamond jewelry, including a bejeweled tiara.

"It would be a nonstop bling-a-thon! I would also have the **perfect friends**, and my **perfect boyfriend** would be a handsome prince, who is utterly in love with me."

But doesn't Melanie already have the perfect wardrobe, hair, and accessories? I think. I guess **every girl** dreams about being *this* kind of princess at one time or another.

Even I have.

"But, Melanie, you already have a great life," I remind her.

Her face lights up and then falls a little.

"You're right." Then Melanie locks her eyes on mine. "Don't you think I would make a *fabulous* princess? Just think about it, Heidi. I would get to live in a palace, **and my face would be on all the money.**"

She waits for my reaction.

Hmmm, should I say something snarky or something nice? I decide on something in between. "You were definitely born to be a princess," I tell her.

She doesn't even suspect I'm being a little sarcastic.

Melanie sighs dreamily. "It's true. I really *was* born to be a royal. Now stay tuned for my fairy-tale ending!"

I give her a thumbs-up.

Somehow we have to get off all this princess talk. I try to change the subject. "So how's your Broomsfield Academy logo coming along?"

Melanie kicks off her fuzzy pink slippers and bounces onto her bed. I'm already sitting on my bed, propped up on pillows.

"I'm still waiting for inspiration to strike me," she replies.

I raise an eyebrow. "But, Melanie, you have to submit it in *three* days!"

Melanie grabs a pink brush from her bedside table. "Don't worry, Heidi, I've *got* this! I do my best work under pressure at the last minute. I'm sure something fabulous is about to pop into my head."

She pulls out her ponytail from her scrunchie and brushes her hair. Then she changes the subject. "I've noticed you've been hanging out a lot with Isabelle lately. What's that all about?"

I wrap my arms around my knees and pull them up to my chest. "Well, it's not *about* anything, Melanie. Isabelle is nice, and we like to hang out together. That's all."

Melanie stops brushing her angelic mane and looks at me. "I heard Isabelle is entering the logo contest. Have you seen any of her ideas?"

Melanie is fishing. "I have, but I've been sworn to secrecy," I tell her. The word "secrecy" makes me shudder.

Melanie begins brushing again. "You two must be getting to be good friends if you already have secrets."

She puts her brush back on the bedside table. "So tell me, what's Isabelle *like,* anyway? She's really hard to get to know."

I stretch out my legs. "She's kind of guarded at first, but once you get to know her, she opens up."

Melanie picks up her social studies packet, which is the same one as mine, the one with the life story of Queen Elizabeth.

"So why do you think Isabelle acts so aloof and mysterious at first?" Melanie asks as she randomly flips through the pages of her packet. **"She's almost a little bit snobby."**

Then she holds up a picture of the British royal family. **"It's not like she's *royalty* or anything."**

Melanie strikes a pose as if she is a queen, with her head held high.

Then she laughs and scrunches up her face and rolls her eyes, as if this idea is *totally* ridiculous.

I gasp because I just can't contain it!

And I can't believe Melanie just said that!

Melanie looks at me suspiciously. "What's wrong, Heidi? Do you *know* something?"

My face flushes. "Uh, no. It's nothing, Melanie. I suddenly realized how late it's gotten—that's all."

But Melanie is onto me.

This girl can smell gossip a mile away.

She gets off her bed and marches
over to mine. She plants both
hands on her hips.

"You're *hiding* something, Heidi Heckelbeck. I *know* it," she says like she's cross-examining me in a courtroom.

"When I said, 'It's not like Isabelle is royalty or anything,' you gasped. And then your face turned pale.

"You *know* something, Heidi. You have a SECRET.

"What is it? *Tell me!*"

I bite my lip and try to think of something to throw Melanie off track, but it's too late.

She's put it all together. I can see it on her face.

Her eyes have grown round, like an owl's. Then she announces her verdict.

"WAIT . . . is Isabelle royalty?

"Is she a PRINCESS?"

I shake my head. I try to deny it every way I know how, but it's hopeless.

Melanie has seen right through me.

It's game over, Heidi. . . .

My secret is out!

FORGET ABOUT IT!

Good work, Heidi!

You just made your worst fear come true! You have successfully betrayed Isabelle! I think.

But did I really?

Melanie dragged this secret out of me.

It's not like I flat-out told her.

She guessed!

And now Melanie knows Isabelle's secret. I'm officially a disloyal friend. This is especially gut-wrenching because Mrs. Kettledrum told us loyalty is the bond for a long-lasting friendship.

"Loyalty" is the word of the month!

And Lucy stressed how important it is too! I totally blew it. I've let my new, and probably soon-to-be-ex, friend down!

Somehow I have to stop Melanie from blabbing Isabelle's secret.

I stand up from my bed and confront my roommate.

"Melanie, you can't tell ANYBODY about Isabelle's secret," I say with as much force as I can.

"She doesn't want ANYONE to know. So PLEASE. I'm BEGGING you. Don't say a word."

Melanie sprays one of her overpowering flower perfumes onto her wrist and laughs. "Oh, zip it, Heidi! It's too late now—you let the cat out of the bag!"

She rubs her wrists together so they'll soak in the perfume. "And besides, being a princess is an amazing secret! Does this mean there's a royal order of witches and wizards? Like a magical monarchy?"

I ball up my fists because I'm SO mad, and Melanie isn't taking me seriously. All she wants is to know *more, more, more*!

Well, I'm *not* going to be the one to tell her. She smirks as if she knows what I'm thinking.

"Well, if you're not going to tell me the whole story,
I know someone who will—*ISABELLE.*"
Melanie sticks her tongue out at me as if to say,
So there!

I follow Melanie to the full-length mirror. She smiles
at herself, like she's closer to being a princess than
ever.

"Melanie, this is none of your business!

"I found out Isabelle's secret by accident, and I promised not to tell. If you say something, you'll ruin my friendship with Isabelle!"

Melanie harumphs as she looks at herself from all sides in the mirror. "Well, you should've thought of that before, Heidi. If you wanted to keep this secret, you would have. But since you're terrible at keeping secrets, now it's mine to tell!"

Then she turns around and looks at me. "And you know what, Heidi? Maybe you should submit a logo after all. It could be a Broomsfield bear with its foot in its mouth." Then she cackles at her own joke.

I glare at Melanie, and all the years of why I couldn't stand her come rushing back.

Sometimes she can be so cruel and harsh.

I cross my arms defiantly. And you know what Melanie does when she sees me getting madder by the minute? She waggles a finger in my face!

"Don't be mad at *ME*, Heidi," she chides. "This is all *your* own doing."

Suddenly my anger turns to shame.

Even if Melanie sort of guessed, I feel so guilty. I need to find a way to make this right.

"And besides," Melanie goes on, "when I *do* reveal Isabelle's secret, she will become the most popular girl in school. And I will be her very best friend. Maybe she can even give me some princess lessons, like Mia in *The Princess Diaries*, though I doubt I'll need them."

I follow Melanie into the bathroom. "Melanie, STOP," I beg. "This is *exactly* why Isabelle doesn't want her secret out. She doesn't want people to be friends with her just because she's a princess.

"And P.S., that strategy didn't work on Mia Thermopolis, either. She could smell a fake friend a mile away."

Melanie splashes water onto her face and dabs her cheeks with a towel. Now she looks at me in the bathroom mirror.

"Isabelle is *nothing* like Mia. Mia was geeky and nerdy before and after she found out she was a princess. Isabelle, on the other hand, is athletic and fashionable, and even the most popular guy in class thinks she's the coolest, without anyone even knowing that she's a princess!

"Come to think of it, it's uncanny how much Isabelle and I have in common. We were meant to be best friends.

"Now stop worrying, Heidi. I'll make Isabelle glad her secret is out. She'll thank me. You'll see."

I shake my head miserably. "Melanie, you have no idea what Isabelle is really like, but I do—and she's NOTHING like you."

Melanie laughs off my comment. "And who are YOU to judge? You've been friends with Isabelle for what, TWO whole days?"

Melanie pushes past me and crawls into bed. "Honestly, Heidi, I'm not trying to be mean. This is more about *my* destiny than it is about you. So don't worry. Everything will be fine.

"I will even tell Isabelle you didn't mean to let me in on her secret. I will just tell her I guessed, because I did! See? It's all good.

"I'm not mad at you or anything. Okay?" She switches off her light, slips on her ridiculous pink silk eye mask, and rests her head on her pillow.

I sure wish she'd wipe that smug, I-know-a-real-princess smile off her face.

MERG!

"Night night, Heidi," she says with fake sweetness.

UGH! That does it!

I storm back into the bathroom and slam the door. I look in the mirror, and all I can see is a traitor. And that's not someone I ever wanted to be!

But *plot twist*! Now I am!

Everything was going so well this week, I think as I begin to brush my teeth. I was becoming a better witch, **and I even made a new friend.**

And now I'm a full-blown mess.

And if somebody was going to find out Isabelle's secret, **why, oh why, did it have to be Melanie?** Anyone else, I could have had a heart-to-heart talk with, and I might even have convinced them to keep the secret. But not oh-I've-wanted-to-be-a-princess-my-whole-life Melanie!

For as long as she has known me, **Melanie always loves it when I slip up.**

I climb into bed and stare at the glow-in-the-dark stars on the ceiling.

I can't stop rehashing what happened and how Melanie found out—and worse, imagining the dreaded fallout that's sure to follow.

How can I get Melanie to keep quiet?

Is there a spell where she loses her voice? Or can't write a note?

Two words: *if only!*

But I have to do *something*!

Then it dawns on me. Maybe I can perform an Emergency Spell on Melanie.

I already successfully unlocked Mrs. Kettledrum's door. And besides, I reason, Mrs. Kettledrum wouldn't have taught me how to cast Emergency Spells if I wasn't meant to use them.

And this is another bona fide emergency. There's absolutely no doubt about that.

So right then and there, I decide to come up with a spell on the spot.

I skip the emergency checklist and grab my flashlight, a pencil, and a notepad from my bedside table.

Then I make up a Forgetting Spell.

As soon as I write down the spell, I begin to feel better. I start to breathe normally again!

I tiptoe over to Melanie's bed.

"Melanie?" I whisper.

This reminds me of our first week at school when I cast some pretty good prank spells on Melanie. But this is nothing like casting a silly prank spell.

This spell is to protect Isabelle and save our friendship.

"Melanie?" I say again, only this time a little louder.

Melanie's breathing remains steady. She's definitely asleep.

And she still has that annoying smile on her face. But it won't be there for much longer.

I hold my flashlight over my notepad and chant my Emergency Spell.

A shower of sparkles shimmers and sifts down onto Melanie's head.

Melanie groans and rolls over.

Fingers crossed that this spell fixes my mess. If not, Isabelle will never speak to me again. I might have to confess my problem to Mrs. Kettledrum, and then she'll probably cancel my advanced magic lessons.

Ugh!

Why, oh why, is everything so hard in middle school?

MiND GAMES

Bling-a-ling-a-ling! Bling-a-ling-a-ling!

Melanie's alarm wakes me up. I squash one of my pillows onto my head.

To say I didn't sleep well is an understatement.

I couldn't stop thinking about the secret and the Forgetting Spell. I hope that Isabelle's secret is completely erased from Melanie's memory.

The tossing and turning all night has left me feeling like Princess Crankypants.

Melanie's feet hit the floor, so I pull the pillow off my head. Time to find out if my spell worked, or if I'm doomed to be a social outcast for the rest of my life at Broomsfield Academy.

It's the moment of truth.

Melanie yawns, stretches, and heads for the bathroom.

"Good morning, Melanie!" I say in the most normal way I know how.

Melanie turns around and smiles at me.

"Good morning!" Then she gives me a funny look. "Um . . . what's your name again?"

I throw back my sheets. "What are you talking about, Melanie? You know very well what my name is!"

Melanie scratches her head. "I'm so sorry. I seem to have forgotten. Who are you again?"

My mouth falls open. "Wait, you really don't know who I am?"

Melanie shrugs and lifts her hands in the air, like she truly doesn't know what's up.

Uh-oh.

"Well, I *know* you're my roommate. That's pretty obvious. I just don't remember you or your name. Silly me!"

I almost fall off the edge of my bed. "My name is Heidi."

It feels **ridiculous** to say that out loud. It's like Melanie is playing dumb, but I know she's not! "Do you remember what we did last night?"

Melanie looks up in thought. "I saw *The Princess Diaries.* What did *you* do?"

I search for an answer. "I did the same thing. You don't remember anything big happening when we got back to this room?"

"I just remember being pretty tired from a busy week," replies Melanie. "Why? What happened?"

I shake my head, dumbfounded. Then Melanie takes a good hard look at me.

"Hey, I love your polka-dot pajamas!" she says without a speck of sarcasm. "They're **supercute!**" Then she smiles warmly.

"Well, I have to get ready. Maybe I'll see you later, *um,* Heidi, right?" She bounces off to the bathroom.

I slap my hands against my cheeks. *So much for forgetting the secret! Melanie doesn't seem to remember me at all!*

OMGosh!

I wonder what ELSE I've erased from Melanie's memory?

I run to the bathroom door. "Melanie, what are you doing today?"

I can hear her tap her toothbrush on the side of the sink. "Well, it's Make-Your-Own-Waffle Saturday, so I'm going to do that. Then I have my piano lesson at eleven. I'm going to sit with Nick and Annabelle at lunch, and then we're going to the boys' soccer game. I'm also going to work on my school logo submission in the art room. How about you?"

I shake my hands wildly in a panic.

But I need to answer her. Calmly, like nothing is wrong. "Oh, I'll probably go to the waffles breakfast too. The rest of my day is wide open. I'll just play it by ear."

Okay, Melanie remembers everything *she's* up to—she just doesn't seem to remember anything about *me*.

This is *bad.*

I wonder if I could get expelled for tampering with Melanie's brain.

What will Mrs. Kettledrum say?

What will my parents say?

What is my problem?

I realize I need to calm down, so I do some quick breath work.

Breathe in. Breathe out. *This will all work out, Heidi,* I tell myself.

And look on the bright side. If Melanie doesn't remember me, *that also means she won't remember finding out Isabelle's secret. See? There's a silver lining here.*

I put my ear to the bathroom door. I can hear the shower. I can also hear Melanie's thoughts, which is what I was hoping for. I listen in on her thinking.

Why can't I remember my roommate's name—or who she is? This is so weird!

I'd better be careful what I say to her.
What if she isn't a witch?

I wonder if I should go to the nurse's office, or maybe I should talk to Mrs. Kettledrum.

I just can't understand why my roommate seems totally unfamiliar to me. Maybe I just need some breakfast.

I step away from the bathroom door and cover my mouth with my hand.

She doesn't even remember I'm a WITCH!

A bottle of shampoo falls onto the shower floor. I hear Melanie set it upright.

"AHA!" Melanie cries. "I've got it!"

What is she talking about now? I wonder. *Did her memory of me and Isabelle's secret come back to her?* I push my ear against the door again.

"Got what?" I shout through the door.

Melanie turns off the water. "I got an idea for my school logo! It just hit me in the shower!"

I move away from the door. "That's great news!" I try to sound enthusiastic.

Melanie opens the door a crack. "Are *you* creating a logo?"

I shake my head. "Nope," I say. "I have other things to work on right now. . . ."

Like fixing the hole I made in your brain!

Melanie struts out of the bathroom in her robe, her hair wrapped in a towel. "You want to go to the cafeteria with me?"

I try not to look too surprised, because I'm not used to Melanie being so nice to me. And I have to admit, I kind of like it. "Thanks, but I still have to shower and get ready. I'll meet you there."

Melanie is long gone when I get out of the shower.

Aahhh, a moment of peace.

I jump into my favorite distressed jean skirt. We're only allowed to wear ripped jeans and skirts on the weekend. Then I pull on a cream-colored, quarter-zip top and my slip-on sneakers. Let's go!

I dash to the cafeteria. Make-Your-Own-Waffle Saturdays are my **favorite** too. I spy an open waffle iron. I grab a pitcher of waffle batter and drizzle it onto the hot grid. Then I shut the lid and wait for the ding. *Doo-de-doo. DING!* I stick a fork into my golden-brown waffle and plop it onto a plate.

Now for toppings! A squirt of whipped cream. A spoonful of strawberries. And a drizzle of maple syrup. On the side I have a cup of hot chocolate with mini marshmallows.

One word: *heaven!*

I sit next to Sunny and Annabelle.

Wait, what's Annabelle doing at our table?

And where's Isabelle?

Oh no! What if Isabelle is sitting with Melanie?

I look over, and sure enough Isabelle and Melanie are sitting together with my low-key crush, Nick.

I wonder what they're talking about?

Did Melanie remember Isabelle's secret on the way to breakfast?

I really hope not!

I turn toward Annabelle. "What are you doing at our table this morning?"

Sunny and Annabelle exchange a look. I guess that sounded a little harsh.

I try to recover. "No, no, I didn't mean it in a *mean* way. I just meant, did Isabelle ask you to swap seats?"

Annabelle shakes her head. "No, Hunter had to get ready for his soccer game, so he left early. Isabelle just sat over at that table for a change—so I guess we did kind of swap seats."

I shovel a forkful of waffle into my mouth and wipe some whipped cream from my lips with a napkin.

"Is something the matter, Heidi?" Sunny asks.

Wow, is it that obvious? I suddenly feel **defensive.** "Why would you think something's the matter?"

Sunny and Annabelle glance at each other again.

"Well, you seem a little jumpy this morning, and you have dark circles under your eyes. And, well, it looks like you forgot to part your hair," Sunny says.

I touch my hair.

Merg!

I was in such a rush that I just ran out of my room without even brushing my hair.

Can this day get any worse?

I set down my fork and decide to fess up. "Well, I did have kind of a rough night," I admit.

And I'm just about to tell my friends what went down, when Melanie passes by our table on the way to the dish drop.

"Hey, Heidi!" she says ultra-cheerfully. "See? I remembered your name this time!"

I smile weakly as Melanie moves on.

Sunny and Annabelle stare at me.

"What was THAT all about?" Sunny asks. "What did Melanie mean when she said, 'I remembered your name this time'?"

I push my plate away. "*We-l-l-l* . . . I kind of put a Forgetting Spell on Melanie. And, *uh*, it sort of backfired, and now, *um*, she doesn't remember me. . . ."

Sunny and Annabelle push their chairs back in shock. They can't believe I'm in yet *another* mess.

To be honest, neither can I.

Annabelle, who is a total rule-follower, is appalled by my behavior. "Heidi, that's a *terrible* thing to do!"

I cover my ears because I can't bear to be called out right now. I feel bad enough as it is!

Thankfully, Sunny says something positive. "Well, maybe Mrs. Kettledrum can help you reverse the spell."

I uncover my ears. "But what if I don't really *want* to reverse it?"

Sunny's mouth drops open. "Of course you have to reverse it, Heidi! What are you *talking* about?!"

I look down. "Well, now that Melanie doesn't know who I am, she's being a lot nicer to me, and I'm not totally sure I want to bring the old Melanie back."

Annabelle and Sunny both roll their eyes.

"But you *have* to make things right," Annabelle insists.

I sigh. "I know, but I don't want to tell Mrs. Kettledrum either. What if she cancels my private magic lessons?"

Sunny shakes her head. "I doubt that will happen, Heidi, because she knows you're still learning."

Obviously.

"And besides, you can't be her first private student to make a mistake."

A *mistake* or *TWO*, if I'm being honest with myself.

My friends have no idea I also swiped my phone from Mrs. Kettledrum's apartment! But to be fair, I put my phone back, so no real harm done, except for another mark on my character.

"Well, I hope you're right, Sunny," I say. "I have a lesson with Mrs. Kettledrum this afternoon, so maybe I'll confess my problem to her then."

My friends look visibly relieved that I'm going to take action and talk to a seasoned witch.

I glance over at Isabelle at the other table.

She smiles and waves at me. I wave back. Isabelle is acting normal, so at least I can be happy about *one* thing—the most important part of my spell worked. Melanie forgot the secret.

But the bad thing is, I'm still in hot water.

One word: *stressed.*

12

FORGET-ME-NOTS

After breakfast Sunny, Annabelle, and I sign up for an optional Saturday spells and potions class. Mrs. Kettledrum is the teacher, and my private lesson is right after the class.

Eek to that!

As soon as I sit down, Mrs. Kettledrum gives me one of her knowing looks. It's the look she gives me when she wants to tell me something by way of her thoughts. It's pretty easy for me to hear Mrs. Kettledrum's thoughts because she knows how to get my attention.

I can hear her as clearly as if she were speaking to me out loud.

I tune in.

Heidi, when class is over, we'll work out this mess with Melanie. Don't worry, everything will be all right. I had no idea you'd need an Emergency Spell so soon!

I nod—just a little—so no one will notice, except for Mrs. Kettledrum. Wow, I can't believe Mrs. Kettledrum already knows what's going on, when I didn't tell her anything yet! I dream of being able to do that one day.

And the best part?

I finally feel some relief, like maybe this whole thing *will* work out.

And if I go back to being the only one at Broomsfield who knows Isabelle's secret, I *know* I'll be able to keep it this time.

There's no way I *ever* want to feel this anxious again.

Plus, the urge to tell Isabelle's secret has faded too—just like Lucy said it would.

Thank goodness!

Mrs. Kettledrum gets up from her desk, and Momo leaps onto her seat. "Okay, Saturday students, are you ready for my special spells and potions class?"

"YES!" we all shout.

Mrs. Kettledrum claps her hands. "Good! Because today we're going to make a potion for *glow-in-the-dark* bubble gum!"

The class hoots and claps, because how cool is THAT?!

Mrs. Kettledrum waits for us to quiet down. "Now let's step into the cauldron room since this potion requires counter space *and* mini cauldrons."

We file into the cauldron room. Sunny, Annabelle, and I sit at a station together. Mrs. Kettledrum passes out bowls filled with little pellets of unflavored gum base.

We pour the pellets into our mini cauldrons to soften them.

After that, we get to pick flavors!

I choose rainbow fruit. Annabelle picks birthday cake. And Sunny chooses lemon meringue pie. Next we sweeten our gum with corn syrup.

And then we add the magical ingredient— the thing that will make our gum glow in the dark!

It's called Mega Magical Fluorescent Food Coloring. It glows even in the light of day!

We squeeze drops of the food coloring into our gum mixture. Then we smoosh it in with our hands.

Squish! Squoosh! Squash!

"This stuff looks radioactive!"

Annabelle exclaims.

We giggle even though we know Mrs. Kettledrum would never let us eat anything toxic.

Once we each have a glowing ball of gum dough, it's time to slice it into cubes. First we sprinkle the counter with confectioners' sugar, so the dough won't stick. Then we roll our gum into logs.

I shape mine into a square log because I want perfect gum cubes, like the ones you can buy at the store. Then we slice our gum into individual pieces. This is so cool!

"Is everyone ready to try their gum?" Mrs. Kettledrum asks.

"YES!" we yell.

Mrs. Kettledrum snaps her fingers and turns out the lights. She snaps her fingers again, and the lights come back on as *black lights.*

"On your mark! Get set! *Chew!*" she cries.

We pop pieces of gum into our mouths. Then we chew, stretch, and blow glow-in-the-dark bubbles!

Under the black lights, the only thing that's visible is our gum, and anything we're wearing that's white. Mrs. Kettledrum puts on music to make it even MORE fun.

We dance around and blow bubbles.

Pop! Crackle! Fssssst!

Sunny sucks in a bubble. I blow a big bubble and hold it for as long as I can. Annabelle grips a wad of gum in her teeth and pulls it straight out of her mouth. The boys blow bubble-gum raspberries, and it sounds like a bunch of whoopee cushions going off.

We chew and dance until our gum grows tough and loses its flavor.

Mrs. Kettledrum passes out bits of paper so we can get rid of our chewed gum. After we clean up, I stay after class to meet with Mrs. Kettledrum.

Sunny and Annabelle give me thumbs-ups as they leave.

Mrs. Kettledrum and I go into her office and sit in our chairs across from each other. Momo hops into my lap again too. **We get right down to work.**

"Okay, Heidi," Mrs. Kettledrum says after I've told her what happened with my Forgetting Spell. **"I want you to repeat the spell you cast on Melanie *exactly* as you said it."**

Luckily, I saved the scrap paper I wrote the spell on. Mrs. Kettledrum taught me early on to **never throw out a spell** because it may come in handy if something goes wrong. I fish the spell out of my backpack and read it out loud.

MELANIE MAPLETHORPE, HEAR, WHAT I SAY!
FORGET ISABELLE'S SECRET BY THE LIGHT OF DAY.
I AM A GOOD WITCH OF KINDNESS AND LOYALTY.
SO FORGET WHAT YOU KNOW ABOUT
SECRETS AND ROYALTY.
ERASE EVERYTHING IN THE ISABELLE CASE.
FORGET THE HORROR, YOU SAW ON MY FACE.
ALL WILL BE FINE—WHEN YOU HEED MY PLEA.
NOW FORGET THE SECRET ABOUT ISABELLE AND ME!

Mrs. Kettledrum holds up her finger. I think she's spotted the problem.

"Heidi, your spell was perfect until the very last line, where you say, 'Now forget the secret about Isabelle and me!' See your wording? You actually asked for Melanie to forget *you*, too."

I puff out my cheeks and blow out the air.

Oh merg! She's right!

Mrs. Kettledrum notices how upset I look. "Not to worry, Heidi. This is a good lesson. It will remind you to be more careful with your spells in the future. Words can be very powerful."

Mrs. Kettledrum gets up and goes to her potions cabinet. She pulls out a clear plastic bag full of tiny dried flowers.

"These flowers are called forget-me-nots," she explains. "I want you to put them on Melanie's pillow after she falls asleep tonight. Then you can chant this spell." Mrs. Kettledrum jots down a spell and hands it to me.

"Will I need to remove the forget-me-nots after the spell?"

Mrs. Kettledrum shakes her head. "The flowers will disappear once the spell has been cast.

"When Melanie wakes up, everything should be back to normal. She'll remember you, but don't worry, she still won't remember Isabelle's secret. I've already taken care of that."

My eyebrows shoot up. "How'd you know about Isabelle's secret?"

Mrs. Kettledrum laughs. "Your spell mentioned 'forget Isabelle's secret.'"

I roll my eyes, because of course.

Duh.

And then I add, "Isabelle told me that the School of Magic staff knows about her family's royal background."

Mrs. Kettledrum smiles. "Oh, that's the secret? Yes, dear, we all know about Isabelle's family history, and you were a good friend to try so hard to protect her secret."

I nod. "I really did try to keep her secret, Mrs. Kettledrum! Melanie is just a good detective, I guess."

Momo barks and jumps off my lap.

Mrs. Kettledrum meets my eye.

"And one last thing, Heidi. I know you came into my apartment and *borrowed* your phone."

My face flushes.

Oh no!

I quickly try to explain. "I was going to ask, but you weren't home."

Mrs. Kettledrum looks at me over the rims of her glasses. "Heidi, you *must* learn to do the right thing under *all* circumstances.

"You're a very good witch, but you do get ahead of yourself sometimes.

"Work on it."

I look down at my shoes. "I'll do better next time."

Mrs. Kettledrum pats my shoulder. "Let's try not to *have* a next time."

Then she smiles. "I know how hard it is, Heidi.

"So much change all at once. A new school, new friends, new secrets, new crushes."

I stare at Mrs. Kettledrum in shock.

"Mrs. Kettledrum, did you just read my mind?" I ask.

Mrs. Kettledrum laughs. "I didn't have to, my dear. I was once in middle school myself, you know. And I remember everything about it. Oh, my memory is very long, Heidi."

Momo yaps to emphasize it.

I know it's important to do the right thing.

The problem is, I just don't know if I can fully master doing the right thing under *every* stressful circumstance.

But I'll definitely try!

Two words: *be good.*

At bedtime I wait for Melanie to fall asleep.

But, unfortunately, I fall asleep first.

I can't help it. I'm pooped after my sleepless night.

Luckily, I wake up at one in the morning.

Ugh.

I haul my sorry bones out of bed, grab my mini flashlight, and shine it into my backpack. I pull out the bag of forget-me-nots and the spell Mrs. Kettledrum gave me, and I turn the flashlight off.

"Hey, Melanie!" I say in my regular daytime voice.

No answer.

Good. That means she's fast asleep.

I shake the dried forget-me-nots into the palm of my hand as I walk over to Melanie's bed. Then I sprinkle them onto her pillow.

She rolls over. I freeze for a second, though I'm pretty sure she's still asleep.

I switch my flashlight back on so I can chant the spell.

A poof of sparkles shimmers over Melanie's head and disappears.

Well, I hope that does the trick,
I think as I tiptoe back to my side of the room.

I fold up the piece of paper with the spell and put it into the bottom of my backpack. I'll return it to Mrs. Kettledrum next time I see her.

I drop the flashlight into my nightstand and dive into bed. **Now it's my turn to forget about _everything_—well, at least until morning. . . .**

Honk-shoo! Honk-shoo!

(That's the sound of me snoring.)

13

AN EVERYDAY PRINCESS

On Sunday morning I sit up in bed and wait for Melanie to wake up, but ugh, she's taking way too long!

I try everything I can think of to rouse her. I cough loudly. I clear my throat.

That girl is still snoring away!

So then I open and close my nightstand drawer, like, five times.

Finally Melanie wakes up!

"Keep it down, Heidi! It's Sunday, and I want to sleep in!" she yells.

I pump my fist.

This is such a *YAY!*

She just called me Heidi *and* yelled at me.

Now I *know* the reversal spell worked, for sure.

"Woo-hoo!" I shout, because I can't contain my joy.

Melanie groans and pulls off her eye mask. "Heidi, why do you have to be SO annoying?"

Then she looks at me more closely, and her eyes narrow. "Wow. Is that your *real* hair, or is that a rat's nest on top of your head?"

I put my hand on my head.

My hair feels a **lot more** frizzball-ish than normal.

But who cares?

I'm in the best mood ever,
because Isabelle's secret is safe
again and Melanie is back to normal.

"Didn't I tell you, Melanie? I'm trying out for
the lead role in *Annie*," I say, just to be silly.

Melanie laughs so hard, she snorts. "You
are hilarious, Heidi."

I grab a fistful of my hair in each hand and hold it
straight out, like Pippi Longstocking. "Yes, I am!"

We both crack up. "So, Melanie, did you finish
your logo?"

Melanie sits up. "I handed it in yesterday
afternoon. I think it's a winner, Heidi.
I'll tell you about it because I
totally trust you."

Wow, I'm glad Melanie trusts me, because she should . . . well, at least most of the time. My intentions are always good—that's for sure. "Thanks, Melanie. I promise not to share your logo idea with anyone."

Melanie tucks a wisp of hair behind her ear. "Okay, good!

"So I took our bear mascot and made it look like a teddy bear, because teddy bears make us feel protected and safe. And just like a kid carrying a teddy bear, we carry our memories of Broomsfield Academy with us wherever we go. My bear also holds a broom over its head in a victory pose—just like the victorious students at Broomsfield Academy." Melanie looks at me expectantly. "So what do you think?"

BROOMSFIELD ACADEMY

I tilt my head to one side and think about her idea for a second.

I love it. It's such a cute idea, but it sounds a little bit young and maybe too cutesy to be a school logo.

I don't tell Melanie this, because it'll crush her excitement, so I tell her something that's also true. "I think that sounds absolutely adorable, Melanie! And your idea is totally original too. I can't wait to see it."

Melanie smiles and twirls her hair with her finger. "Thanks, Heidi, that means a lot."

The rest of Sunday feels like a real day off. I practice my meditation, play Four Square, and write my "If I Were a Princess for a Day" essay.

If I Were a Princess for a Day
By Heidi Helena Heckelbeck

Once upon a time my princess-for-a-day storyline might have gone like this:

There once was a gorgeous girl named Heidi who got to be a princess for a day.

Princess Heidi had long flowing strawberry-blond hair and a beautiful smile. She also had the most enviable wardrobe in all the kingdom, along with a sparkling diamond tiara.

On that one special day, the princess was beloved by all her friends, and her boyfriend was, of course, a seriously handsome prince named Prince Nicholas.

On the afternoon of being princess for a day, Princess Heidi and Prince Nicholas rode their horses until sunset. In the evening Princess Heidi held a ball in her palace for all her friends and admirers.

When the guests arrived, Princess Heidi made a grand entrance from the top of a long winding stairway. She slowly descended the stairs in a shimmering emerald-green ball gown. Everyone gasped at her stunning beauty.

Then she mingled and danced with her friends all night. At the stroke of midnight Princess Heidi returned to her regular, everyday life in her not-so-royal town of Brewster.

Record scratch!

Like I said before, that's how I *used* to imagine being a princess for a day, but not anymore. I'm *done* with that idea.

And to be honest, I wouldn't actually *want* to be a princess for a day. I want to be a princess *every* day. I'd like to be the kind of princess I am right now, with all my imperfections.

And each day I will strive to work toward grand and royal goals! I want to be a princess known for her good work, and not just a beauty queen with a ridiculously expensive wardrobe.

Don't get me wrong. I do want to look my best, but not to make others envy me or be my friend just because I'm a princess. I want people to like me because I'm a loyal and dependable friend.

I know I have a lot of work to do to be an everyday princess, and I may make a ton of mistakes along the way. But I'll learn from them all, no matter how hard it might be, because I am the princess of my own story, and my happily ever after is today, tomorrow, and every day after that.

The End

P.S. I'm not opposed to a Prince Charming.

HH

A TRUE PRINCESS

On Monday I hand in my social studies essay.

In the afternoon we have another school-wide assembly.

Mrs. Kettledrum is going to announce the winner of the logo contest!

I sit with my squad: Melanie, Isabelle, Hunter, Sunny, and Annabelle.

And guess what?

Nick joins us too!

I'm swooning.

This week has been so busy that I haven't had much time to think about Nick.

But I have time now!

Crush ON!

I spy Natalie and Jenna sitting in the row beside us.
I give Natalie a thumbs-up, because I know
she's worked superhard on her logo.
She gives me a thumbs-up back.

"Did all of you submit a logo for the competition?"
Nick asks. And I swear he looks right at
me when he asks this.

Melanie, Sunny, Annabelle, and Isabelle all nod. But
I shake my head, and this makes him ask
more questions . . . about me!

I take this as an invitation to speak.

This is your time, Heidi, I think.

"I'm not really great at art. I'm more into
writing," I explain. "Like, uh, poems and stuff."

Good one, Heidi. I hear Sunny's voice, and I shoot her a look to let her know I heard her and also to thank her for the compliment.

I'm getting good at code language so that I don't accidentally tell a non-magical student about the School of Magic.

"That's really cool, Heidi. I'm not any good at art either.

"I also didn't submit a logo for the competition. But I used the time I would have spent on coming up with one to do some research about the original Broomsfield Academy logo. I really like history."

This makes Nick blush a bit, like he's a little embarrassed.

Is he blushing because he's talking to me?!

Okay, calm down, Heidi! I pull myself back to earth.

"History is really cool," I say. "Did you find out anything interesting?"

"Actually I did!" he says with a big smile. "It turns out that some people thought the logo was a hidden message of some kind, but I couldn't find out what that message was.

"The research kind of just stopped there. Really weird, but *super-interesting*. Don't you think?"

This time Nick's words don't give me butterflies in my stomach. Instead they make my stomach feel like it's about to fall out of my body!

Nick might end up researching his way to discovering the secret of the School of Magic!

Just then Mrs. Kettledrum and Momo walk to the podium.

If I didn't know any better, Nick's research stalling was one of Mrs. Kettledrum's ways of not letting the non-magical students get too close to our secret!

"Hello, students! Who's ready to see our new school logo?" she begins.

I use this as an excuse to end our history conversation. "Oh, look, Mrs. Kettledrum is going to announce the winner!" And just like that, Nick looks to the stage.

That was close!

The whole student body whistles and cheers. Melanie pinches me. I pinch her back, but I secretly want Isabelle to win.

Shhhh.

Isabelle did a very simple and very cool logo of a bear pawprint in a circle, with a broom leaning up against the circle. It said "Broomsfield" above the pawprint and "Academy" underneath.

It was simple and elegant.

Perfect.

Mrs. Kettledrum turns toward a large lit screen as she announces the winning logo. She holds a remote in one hand and a microphone in the other.

"It was a close call between two students—a first-year student and an upperclassman. Let's have a round of applause for Natalie Nguyen and Isabelle Summer!"

We all clap, whistle, and bounce up and down in our seats. Even Melanie is excited, which is amazing, because her logo didn't get picked.

Isabelle turns to me with her fingers crossed on one hand. Hunter is holding her other hand.

Aw, that is so cute!

"Are you ready to hear our winner?" Mrs. Kettledrum asks.

Isabelle and I give each other an intense look of anticipation. The kind of look you would give your friend when you're approaching the top of a roller coaster.

"YES!" everyone shouts.

Then Mrs. Kettledrum clicks the remote and announces, "And our winner is: Natalie Nguyen! With first-year student Isabelle Summer as the runner-up!"

We all gasp and cheer.

Natalie's logo is an enchanted two-way logo.

To the magical students, it's a bear riding a broom and wearing a witch's hat. They can also see what the non-magical students see: a bear leaning on a broom, like he's finished his work for the day.

It's brilliant!

I'm so happy for Natalie. I hope Isabelle isn't too sad that she didn't win.

But Isabelle isn't sad at all.

She's cheering for Natalie!

"Wow! Can you believe I was a runner-up to an upperclassman?" Isabelle exclaims. "That is SO cool!"

I squeal and jump up to hug Isabelle. It *is* pretty cool. Hunter hugs Isabelle too.

Then I turn to Melanie. "Hey, Melanie. I'm really sorry your logo didn't win."

Melanie nudges me with an elbow. "Don't worry. I'm happy for Natalie *and* Isabelle.

"To be honest, everything's always come so easily to me until I got to Broomsfield Academy. It makes me realize I'm surrounded by a lot of really talented people, including you, Heidi. I'm going to have to work at everything a lot harder from now on."

I throw my arms around Melanie, because that was, by far, **the nicest thing she's *ever* said to me, and she's not even under a spell! I'll take it!**

"You're so talented too, Melanie. I think we all have to bring our best game to Broomsfield."

Melanie laughs. **"You're not kidding!"**

As we file out of the auditorium, Isabelle tugs my sleeve. "Do you have time to come back to my room right now? I want to give you something."

I look at Isabelle like, *What more could you possibly have to give me?*

She's already given me a purple headband, a hat, a piece of her artwork made just for me, a super-big secret, and her friendship.

But hey, I'm open!

"Sure!" I say, and we walk back to Dreamwood together.

When we get to Isabelle's room, she goes into her totally unbelievable walk-in closet and comes back with a blue velvet bag. She hands it to me. "This is to say thank you for keeping my secret."

My eyes grow wide. "But, Izzy, you don't need to give me a present! Keeping a secret is just something friends do!"

Isabelle shakes her head. "Not *my* kind of secret.

"Most people would've blabbed that secret all over school, but not you, Heidi, and I really appreciate it. Now go ahead and open it!"

I loosen the strings on the bag and reach inside. It feels like jewelry!

It is!

I pull out a beautiful silver tiara with glittering crystal stones.

It's *exquisite*!

"Isabelle, this is *too* much! I can't accept such a huge gift!" I tell her.

Isabelle clasps her hands together. "Of course you can, Heidi! I want you to have it because a trustworthy friend is a true princess."

Tears well up in my eyes.

If she only knew what her so-called trustworthy friend went through this past week.

"Thank you, Princess Isabelle. I'll treasure it always."

As I walk back to my room, I feel as if I'm floating on air.

Life can get messy, but there's always something beautiful just around the corner, I think.

You just have to hang in there.

In my room I sit on my bed and admire my sparkly tiara.

Right on cue Melanie breezes into the room, and her eyes lock on the tiara.

One word: *predictable.*

"Nice tiara, Heidi," she says, walking straight to her full-length mirror.

"Aren't you a little old to be playing dress-up?"

I guess she couldn't be nice forever, I think. *Otherwise she just wouldn't be Melanie!*

Poor Melanie has no idea that I can hear exactly what she's thinking right now, and it's all about me and the tiara.

I wonder what Heidi's title would be if SHE were royalty, Melanie thinks. *Princess Messy Hair? Heidi, Queen of Striped Tights?*

Melanie chuckles to herself as she walks into the bathroom. The door clicks shut, and she turns on the shower. I chuckle too, because I actually like this Melanie much better than the sweet syrupy one who forgot who I was.

Two words: *good riddance!*

I sit down at my desk.

Then I pull out a piece of Aunt Trudy's stationery. I choose a card outlined in purple.

Time to write my beloved Lucy a letter!

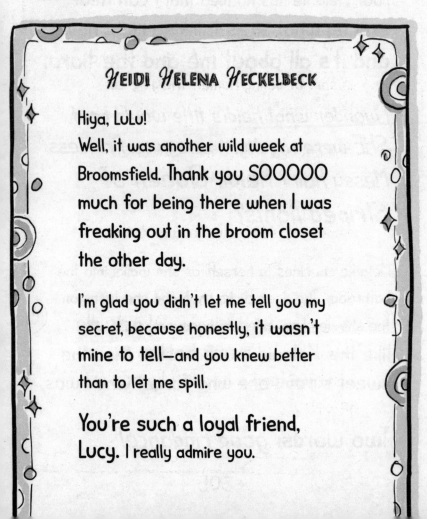

HEIDI HELENA HECKELBECK

Hiya, LuLu!
Well, it was another wild week at Broomsfield. Thank you SOOOOO much for being there when I was freaking out in the broom closet the other day.

I'm glad you didn't let me tell you my secret, because honestly, it wasn't mine to tell—and you knew better than to let me spill.

You're such a loyal friend, Lucy. I really admire you.

And thanks to you I was able to keep the secret. You were right (as always)! The feeling that I had to tell somebody *did* die down after a few days, and now I know I won't slip up. I would never want to betray a new friend—or an old friend, either.

By the way, LuLu, you would love my new friend Isabelle! She's the one who is sort of dating Hunter. They're an item now.

And Izzy and Hunter are perfect for each other. They're both so awesome—not to mention smart and athletic. Isabelle is also really good at drawing and fashion.

She even gave me some cool accessories—a hat (apparently hats are very me! Lol! *NOT*), a new purple headband, and a beautiful piece of jewelry.

HEIDI HELENA HECKELBECK

I also made friends with an upperclassman this week named Natalie. She's best friends with my RA, Jenna. Their friendship reminds me so much of ours, more than you'll ever know! Natalie and Jenna have been friends since elementary school—just like *us*.

And in Crush News: **There's a boy I like named Nick Lee. I danced with him at the Halloween party.** And this time I'm totally following your advice. I'm going to be myself with him no matter what.

I'll keep you posted, of course!

How are things with YOU? Have you met anyone cute since I've been gone? Started any new hobbies? Fill me in, LuLu Kins!

Hey, and maybe one weekend you can come to visit Broomsfield? I'd want to show you around. I know you'll see why I love it here so much. I wish YOU could go here too! What a *happily ever after* THAT would be!

I'm off to get ready for bed, but I'll write again soon. Miss you TONS!

Your BFF always,
Heidi Kins XOXO

I fold up the letter, put it into an envelope, and address it to Lucy.

I leave my room and start to walk to the mail room to buy some stamps and mail the letter. And who should I meet on the way there but Nick!

"Hey, Heidi," he says. "Where are you headed?"

I hold up my envelope. "Just to the mail room," I say.

"Oh, okay," Nick says. "I'll walk with you if you want."

"Oh, sure," I reply.

I am trying to be cool, but I can't help myself. I am grinning like a big goofball.

"What are you smiling at?" Nick asks.

"Oh, nothing!" I say a little too quickly. "I guess I'm just in a good mood."

Now Nick is grinning.

"Okay. Now what are *you* smiling about?" I ask.

Nick shrugs. "I guess seeing you smile put me in a good mood," he says.

Then his cheeks turn pink.

Is he *blushing*?

"You have a really nice smile," he tells me. "I don't know how to explain it. It's almost . . . kind of *magical.*"

Three words: *Best. Compliment. Ever.*

I can't wait to write to Lucy again!

ABOUT THE AUTHOR

Wanda Coven has always loved magic. When she was little, she used to make secret potions from smooshed shells and acorns. Then she would pretend to transport herself and her friends to enchanted places. Now she visits other worlds through writing. Wanda lives with her husband and son in Colorado Springs, Colorado. They have three cats: Hilda, Agnes, and Claw-dia.

ABOUT THE ILLUSTRATOR

Anna Abramskaya was born in Sevastopol, Ukraine. She graduated from Kharkiv State Academy of Design and Arts in 2006. Then she moved to the United States, where she's currently living in the beautiful city of Jacksonville, Florida. Anna has loved art since she was little and has tried different materials and techniques. The process of creation and seeing beauty in the simple things around her always brings her joy and the wish to share that feeling with everyone. Anna wants to believe that art can help bring more love into people's hearts. Find out more at AnnaAbramskaya.com.

Love witches, magic and pranks?
Look out for more books
in the bestselling series!